THE TIME-TRAVELLING CAT
and the
GREAT VICTORIAN STINK

Other Titles by Julia Jarman

THE TIME-TRAVELLING CAT
and the
GREAT VICTORIAN STINK

JULIA JARMAN

Andersen Press • London

First published in 2010 by
Andersen Press Limited
20 Vauxhall Bridge Road
London SW1V 2SA
www.andersenpress.co.uk

British Library Cataloguing in Publication Data available.

ISBN 978 1 84939 019 4

Printed and bound in Great Britain by CPI Bookmarque,
Croydon CR0 4TD

To Peter, my engineer

Chapter 1

There was blood on Ka's ear.

'How did that happen, puss? Where have you been?' Topher Hope was stretched out on the sofa and his lovely cat was curled up on his stomach. *Rrrrrrrrrr. Rrrrrrrrrrrr.* She purred as he stroked the golden fur between her ears.

'A r-r-rat? Is that what you're saying?'

He couldn't be sure if she was saying anything. She might simply be purring, for she behaved like an ordinary cat most of the time. But she had just returned from a night away and he knew she'd been time travelling.

'I said, where have you been? Where did you go?' Topher thought about moving upstairs to his bedroom where his computer was set up. Then Ka might press the keyboard with her paw, as she'd done before, spelling out a word, showing him where and *when* she'd been. Already she'd been to ancient Egypt and several other eras – and so had he in search of her.

He leaned forward to sniff her fur. 'Poo! Have you been visiting the stables?' There was a faint whiff of something smelly. *Horse manure*, he thought. Molly, his stepmum, sometimes took Tally, his little sister, for riding lessons so he recognised the pong.

Rrrrrrrrr-rat. Rrrrrrrrrr-rat.

That was definitely what Ka's purring sounded like.

'I think you should wash yourself.'

But Ka just wanted to sleep. Topher wondered whether he should bathe her ear, or even take her to the vet's. Couldn't you catch horrible diseases from rats? But the blood was dry and she didn't seem ill, so he reached for the worksheet he was supposed to be reading.

Your history topic next term will be Britain since Victorian times. We would like you to research some aspects of 19th- and 20th-century British history for your holiday homework.

Holiday homework, what a cheek!

Task 1. Research and write about one famous Victorian. Write three paragraphs:
Facts about their life
Why they are famous
How they influenced their own time and our lives today

There was a pile of books beside the sofa. Molly had taken him to the library to get them, so he could get the work done at the beginning of the holiday. He'd wanted to get it over with, and now was probably a good time. Rain was running down the conservatory windows though it was supposed to be summer.

Rrrrrrrrr. Rrrrrrrrrrrrr. Ka stretched out so she was facing him and opened her eyes.

'I wish you'd been to Victorian times and met someone famous. You could have saved me a lot of work.'

'*Did.*'

Clear as anything. She spoke. One word. Topher saw her pink mouth open and close.

'Say that again, Ka.'

But she didn't. She curled back up, and he began to worry. When Ka went time travelling she was often in terrible danger. So was he when he went with her. People in the past were often cruel to animals and children. Best not to think about it.

He opened one of the books about Queen Victoria. Her picture was on the cover and she looked fat and disapproving. She'd reigned for sixty-four years, with the help of her husband, Prince Albert, till he died of a terrible disease.

Loads of people died of diseases in Victorian times, even in the royal palaces, mostly because the water supply was contaminated – by poo. Well, the book called it 'faeces' and 'excrement' and 'sewage' but he knew what all these words meant.

There was a whole chapter headed 'Health and Hygiene', but it should have been called 'Dirt and Diseases'. Topher learned that even royal palaces smelled disgusting because all the royal doodahs were stored underneath the floor.

'Yuck.'

It was the same in rich people's houses. At least poor people had outside 'privies', even if several houses did have to share. *Their* poo went into a hole in the ground called a cesspit. The system worked – sort of – when the pits were emptied regularly. Night soil men carted it away and sold it to farmers who used it as manure for their fields. But it all went wrong when the towns got overcrowded and the cesspits overflowed – into the streets. Rich people's new flushing toilets added to the problem by increasing the volume of waste. In those days open sewers ran down the middle of the streets.

'Double yuck!'

There were underground sewers too. All of them were supposed to carry the poo away, first to the rivers, then to the sea. The word sewer actually came from seaward. Interesting, but – oh dear! – it got more disgusting. Victorians got their water from the rivers, so they drank water *with sewage in it*! Poor people got it straight from the river. Rich people bought what they thought was clean water from water companies who sieved river water by passing it through sand. In those days they didn't know about invisible germs and bacteria and stuff.

'Triple yuck, Ka. And you do pong a bit. I'm going to wash my hands.'

Tipping her off his knee as gently as he could, he got up and went to the bathroom. When he got back he was pleased to see that Ka was cleaning herself too. Though, of course, she was swallowing what she licked off. Cats – they were beautiful and disgusting at the same time, even Ka, the loveliest, cleverest cat in the world. Best not to think about the disgusting bits.

'And best not to go time travelling, Ka. Stay at home, right?'

But she went out later that morning, and wasn't back by tea time when his dad and Molly came home from work. Tally was with them. Two years old now, her hair, black like Molly's, was spattered with paint and her hands were full with the pictures she'd done at nursery. She said one of them was for Ka and set off to find her, singing, 'Pussy cat, pussy cat, where have you been?'

Topher followed Tally upstairs into his bedroom, where he too hoped he'd find his cat sleeping on the bed.

But she wasn't. Instead her statue was on his bedside table and Topher felt himself go shivery. Bad news. That meant she'd gone time travelling.

Tally picked up the statue and frowned. 'Ka?'

'Y-yes.' Because the statue *was* her. Sort of. It looked like her. Well, the colours were the same – gold flecked with black and white – but it was made of stone. It turned back into Ka, became a real cat, when she returned from her time travels. And Tally was probably the only person who would believe him if he told her. Little kids believed in magic. Even his best friend, Ellie, hadn't believed him when he'd tried to explain. *He* wouldn't have believed it if he hadn't seen it happening.

His mum had given him the statue before she died, and one night it had come to life, become Ka. Since then she had turned back into a statue several times and he knew now what that meant. When Ka was away, in *this* time she became a statue made of sardonyx, a gold-coloured stone with flecks of black and white in it. When she returned – it took several amazing minutes to happen – she turned into a cat with exactly the same colouring. Exactly the same, right down to the glossy black key-like mark on her forehead. His mum had brought the statue back from Egypt and this strange symbol was the ankh, the ancient Egyptian sign of everlasting life.

Later, when he went to bed, Topher picked up the book about Queen Victoria again. He'd decided that she would be the famous person he'd write on for his homework. She was so rich she had several palaces – that wasn't surprising – but she still wiped her bum on newspaper, when she was living at Windsor Castle anyway. That was because Prince Albert had started a campaign against waste, to save money.

Writing a paragraph of facts about Queen Victoria would be no trouble at all. He'd have to choose his words carefully though. No bums or poo. His teacher was almost as prim as the Victorians.

Why she was famous would be easy too. The book said that when she died in 1901 she was the most famous person on Earth. She was queen, not just of Britain but of a huge empire covering half the world. And she broke records for reigning for such a long time.

How she influenced her own times might be harder to write about, but Queen Victoria had certainly tried. So had Prince Albert, who was all for modernisation. It was his idea to have The Great Exhibition to show off all the new Victorian inventions. He loved machines and lots were invented in this period. It was, the book said, the Age of Progress. Not for everyone though. Poor children had a terrible time because they had to work –

in factories, down mines, up chimneys and even in the sewers.

Reading about the sewers suddenly reminded Topher of Ka's smell and her torn ear. Had a rat really bitten it? *Come home, Ka.*

When it went dark, he lay watching the statue, longing to see the glow that meant she was starting to come back. But it stayed dull and he was filled with a sense of foreboding.

Chapter 2

Ka didn't come back that night.

When Topher woke up, the statue was still there and the day outside looked dull. A mist hung over the garden pond. The only good thing was that he'd finished his homework by lunch time, so he was free. But he didn't *feel* free. It was weird; he felt there was something he ought to be doing, but he didn't know what. He'd spent the last few weeks longing for the summer holidays to begin. Now he couldn't think of anything he wanted to do.

Except find Ka.

He wasn't hungry either and he hadn't even noticed until he got an email from Ellie, headed 'Food, glorious food', reminding him that he hadn't eaten yet that day. Tomorrow Topher was going to stay with Ellie for a week, and her email was to tell him that she had lots of stuff planned for his visit including tickets to go and see *Oliver!*

Ellie lived in north London. They'd been neighbours and school friends, till his dad married Molly and they moved, first to Cambridge then Chichester.

Thinking that he ought to be packing, Topher found his biggest backpack, took it to his bedroom and made a start. While he was doing this, Ellie emailed again to ask if he was going to be bringing Ka with him.

He took a break and replied, telling her he didn't know.

She emailed back saying, *Make up your mind.* Her mum wanted to know if she should buy extra cat food for the week.

Trying to be optimistic about the fact that Ka would return soon, Topher went into the attic to get the cat basket. Ka hated it but she didn't like being on a lead either. Usually he went to London by car with the rest of the family, but this time he was going on the train by himself. A cat on the loose probably wouldn't be allowed, he thought, even a well-behaved cat like Ka. Besides, he might lose her on a crowded train.

If she returned in time to go.

Topher spent most of the morning in his bedroom willing the statue to come to life. But the more he stared at it the duller it looked, so he decided to leave it alone on the watched-kettle principle.

Outside in the garden it was sunny, but he could hear distant thunder and he could see dark clouds rolling towards him. He suddenly felt hot and shivery at the same time. Was he getting a cold? Or was he tired because he'd spent half the night awake watching the statue?

To pass the time he filled the empty bird feeders on the willow tree that drooped into the pond and gave the goldfish some food. Then, deciding that he really should eat something, he went back inside to make a sandwich for his lunch.

Ka, where are you?

The house always felt emptier and colder when she wasn't there.

When he went upstairs the statue was still on his bedside table. Yawning, he lay down and held the cold stone against his forehead. It did make him feel cooler, but he couldn't help thinking about some of the places Ka had travelled to and the dangers she'd faced. She'd been in constant danger in Tudor times as they thought cats were witches in disguise. The Romans loved cats, but the tribes they'd conquered didn't. The Aztecs...

Eventually he must have fallen asleep because he woke to find Molly standing by him looking concerned.

'Are you OK, Topher?' She put her hand on his forehead. 'You feel hot.'

'I've got a bit of a headache.' His head was *pounding*.

'You don't usually fall asleep during the day. I'll get you some aspirin.'

His dad didn't help when he came in, saw the book by the bed and started droning on about the Victorians. 'They'd have given you a bit of willow bark to chew on if you had a headache in those days. Know that? That's where aspirin comes from. Mind you, they might have started manufacturing it by then, in factories. Or they'd have given you opium. A lot of the Victorians were addicts...'

Fortunately Molly returned carrying a glass. 'It's soluble aspirin. Drink it up. You've got to be well to go to London tomorrow.'

'I don't want to go.' He'd made up his mind.

'Why on earth not? You love staying with the Wentworths.'

'Ka's gone AWOL.'

10

'So? She often does, but she'll come back and we'll look after her while you're not here.'

How could Topher say he had this feeling that Ka was in desperate trouble? That she was in some other time where animals weren't treated as well as they are now? He just knew he didn't want to go to London without Ka. He wouldn't enjoy it. He'd worry too much. And what if she needed him? He had to be able get onto his computer to see if she'd left any messages.

Later that night he checked to see if Ka had got in touch, but she hadn't, so he decided to stay awake and watch the statue again.

To pass the time he read about more famous Victorians. There were some really useful ones who improved people's lives by doing things to stop diseases.

There was Florence Nightingale. Well, he'd heard about her improving hospitals by making them cleaner, but there were lots more people he'd never heard of.

There was an amazing man called Dr Snow who actually discovered that sewage in drinking water caused a disease called cholera. Most people, including Florence Nightingale, didn't believe him. So thousands of people kept dying from it. Most people thought it was bad, smelly air – which they called a *miasma* – that caused diseases.

Dr Snow was also Queen Victoria's doctor and when she was having her fourth baby he gave her a gas called chloroform. She hated having babies because it hurt so much, but with chloroform it didn't. The gas put her to sleep. She was so thrilled not to have suffered that she told everyone about it, helping to make anaesthetics respectable. Till then the Church said pain in childbirth was a good thing! Weird! So Queen Victoria was influential there too.

'But I still think Dr Snow deserves to be more famous than the queen, don't you, Ka?' For a moment he forgot she wasn't there.

'Is she back then?' Molly was standing in the doorway.

'No, er...' Topher felt a bit stupid, caught talking to himself.

Molly closed the curtains, darkening his bedroom. 'Stop reading now and try and get a good night's sleep.'

He tried, but it was hard because he had this feeling that Ka wasn't too far away. And he was right because when he woke in the middle of the night there were circles of light, two of them, on the opposite wall and the eyes of the statue were gleaming. That was always the first sign that Ka was on her way home.

'Ka.' He said her name.

But she couldn't hear him. Not yet. She was still stone, still coming back to life bit by bit. It was as if some force were breathing life into her. First her eyes, then the rest of her head began to glow. Then the surface of the stone started to glimmer and shimmer. A ripple began at the tips of her ears and ran through to her long tail, which was wrapped around her seated body. He could feel the heat from the statue, feel her trying to return.

'Come on, Ka.'

The circles on the wall moved from left to right as the cat's head shifted from side to side. The surface glowed more brightly. As she got brighter and brighter, hotter and hotter, the circles faded, disappeared in the general shine and her shape appeared on the wall, a shimmering shadow. Now she looked like molten rock. A cat-shaped fire. He feared she might actually burst into flames.

Come on, Ka.

He willed her to return to him. Quickly. When, *when* would the rock turn to fur? Topher waited and it didn't happen. He began to worry. This was different from before. Always, *always* by this time stone had started to become fur again. But still the statue smouldered. Still it shimmered and rippled. Ka was striving to come home. Topher was sure of it. *What* was stopping her? Her mouth opened and closed but no sound came out. Opened and closed again as if she were crying.

Come on, Ka.

He watched transfixed, willing her to come back to life. For a moment he thought she was. He thought molten stone was becoming fur, but the ripples slowed, the shimmers calmed, the glow dulled. The fur didn't come. Whiskers didn't spring from Ka's face as they had before. Her pointed ears didn't become velvet soft. Instead the statue became still. It was as if she were trapped inside it.

'Where are you, Ka? Where are you?'

There was no reply, and when he touched the stone it was cold.

Chapter 3

Topher got to sleep but woke early and instantly remembered what had happened during the night. He felt for the statue. Cold. Lifeless.

'Come back to me, Ka. Come back. Come back.'

Already he felt hot and sweaty again though he'd thrown off the duvet in the night. It was the weather, he thought. Another hot day was brewing. He was worried, not ill. That's what he told himself anyway as he pushed open the window and scanned the silent garden. Where was Ka? *When* was Ka? He couldn't stop thinking about her. Couldn't stop feeling that she was suffering. That she needed him. But what should he do about it? He caught sight of his packed bag. Should he go to London or stay at home? If only Ka would return right now, so he could sit down at his computer with her on his knee and say 'Where have you been?' Would she do it on Ellie's computer? If she would he could take the statue with him to London.

'Are you packed?' His dad peered round the door. 'You're catching the first cheap train, aren't you? That means we should leave here at nine.'

Maybe it wasn't so early. His dad was already carrying a tray of tea for Molly, her Saturday-morning treat. He'd obviously programmed going to the station into his day. He and Molly both seemed to have forgotten Topher hadn't been well the day before.

'And Mrs Wentworth and Ellie are meeting you at the other end? And you've got to grips with your new mobile so you can ring if there are any hitches?'

'Yes – to both,' Topher answered, making up his mind to take the statue of Ka, but not in his backpack. He chose what to wear more carefully than usual, found a jacket with a big pocket and slipped the statue into that.

As his dad drove him to Chichester station Topher kept his hand on the statue. Kept it there for the whole of the train journey too, not knowing what to hope. He desperately wanted Ka to come back to life, but couldn't help thinking it would be better if she waited till he'd arrived at Ellie's. The carriage was full, and the sudden appearance of a cat would cause comment, even if people didn't notice her actually coming to life.

Fortunately he was on a through train, so he didn't need to worry about changing, but he did need to make sure he got off at the right station. Victoria Station.

Named after the queen he supposed, as he stepped onto the busy platform. Did she know she had a station named after her, he wondered?

A shout broke into his thoughts. 'Topher! We're over here!' And there was Ellie behind the ticket barrier waving both hands madly. Her long dark hair was tied back, unusual for her. She was with her mum and two younger brothers, Luke and Russell the Brussel. The boys pretended to be sick when Ellie greeted him at the other side of the barrier with a hug.

'Shut up, you two,' said Mrs Wentworth. 'I'm afraid we must hurry, Topher. We're in the short-term parking.'

Mr Wentworth was in the people carrier listening to the cricket. 'Hi, Topher, hope you don't mind but we're going to do a bit of a tour before we go home. The boys have got to do a project on the sights of London.' He drove round Victoria Square, Topher noticed, and then turned into Victoria Street. *Victoria.* You couldn't get away from her.

Mr Wentworth drove past Westminster Abbey, pointing it out to the boys, then the Houses of Parliament. They turned left onto Victoria Embankment. The River Thames, dotted with pleasure cruisers, oozed along beside them, and Mr Wentworth became very animated. 'Couldn't have come along here two hundred years ago, or even a hundred and fifty, unless we were in a boat. This would all have been under water then, part of the river. The embankment wasn't built till 1874 by—'

'*BASIL BRUSH!*' Luke and Russell and Ellie shouted together. They had obviously heard this spiel before.

'Shut up, you morons.' Mr Wentworth was unfazed. 'Topher might just be interested. Yes, Topher? You're interested in history, aren't you?'

'Spare us, Dad,' Ellie yawned.

But he ignored his daughter's plea. 'Bazalgette,' he said, 'B-A-Z-A-L-G-E-T-T-E, Joseph Bazalgette. Remember that name. He saved more lives than Florence Nightingale ever did, but hardly anyone has heard of him. An unsung hero.'

'Florence Nightingale did found the nursing profession, darling. Before she took charge only a few drunken women looked after sick people,' Mrs Wentworth said.

'Why isn't Bazalgette famous?' asked Topher politely.

'Creep.' Ellie poked him, and Topher started to say he was doing a project on Queen Victoria. But Mr Wentworth was on a roll.

'Because Joseph Bazalgette didn't have a pretty face. Because what he did is mostly under the ground. Under where we are now,' said Mr Wentworth. The car had stopped at traffic lights. 'And because what he did wasn't the sort of thing polite people talked about then. Still don't. Bazalgette built the sewers, a vast network of huge pipes. They're still under our feet, still taking away all the sewage – to filtration plants now – so it doesn't contaminate the water we drink.'

'And that stopped the cholera epidemics that regularly wiped out thousands of people,' said Ellie, in a not-too-bad imitation of her dad.

Well, perhaps Mr W did go on a bit, but he was interesting. Topher wondered if Mr Bazalgette knew Dr John Snow, who discovered the cause of cholera.

'Be-cause chol-er-a was caused by poo in the wa-ter,' chanted Luke as if he too had heard this information a hundred times before.

Topher started to feel hot and sick again. Was it travel sickness, the petrol fumes or all the talk of poo? He clutched the statue in his pocket and thought of taking it out and putting it against his burning forehead. But then he imagined Ellie or one of her brothers saying, '*What are you doing? What have you brought that for?*' so he didn't.

The car stopped at a busy junction. Concentrating on what was outside, Topher read the name of the road on the side of a building. Queen Victoria Street. Was *everything* in London named after the queen?

'The Gherkin,' said Ellie, pointing to a tall purple building shaped like a gherkin. 'I wonder what she'd have thought of that.'

'Who?' said Luke.

'Queen Victoria. Topher's doing a project on her.'

Done. I've done it. He didn't bother to say it, because he was still feeling sick.

'Why do the queen, Topher?' Mr Wentworth turned to look at him. 'Why not do someone who really made a difference to ordinary people's lives? Do one of the great engineers, Brunel, or one of the Stephensons or even—'

'*BASIL BRUSH!*' yelled the boys again, and Topher's head pounded.

It was getting hotter.

He was getting hotter.

The statue was heating up in his pocket. Could it be coming to life? Topher dismissed the thought. It never happened in the day time. Never happened when there were other people around. More likely it was absorbing the warmth from his over-heating body. He was glad when the car started again and Mr Wentworth turned left, heading for Archway.

They drove past his old house in Arburton Road on

the way to the Wentworths'. It was in a terrace of houses with a higgledy-piggledy roofline and chimney pots shaped like royal crowns. Victorian houses, three storeys high, they had cellars below street level. Some houses had stained-glass windows. The Wentworths' house in Cheverton Road did too.

'Topher, your room's the usual one at the top – in the servants' quarters,' laughed Mrs Wentworth as she opened their door.

'Next to mine,' said Ellie. 'That's what they think children are for – servants.'

'I'm not.' Luke shot past his sister into the kitchen at the back of the house, closely followed by Russell.

'Race you to the top!' Ellie started running upstairs, but to his shame, Topher couldn't keep up. He really didn't feel well.

And another thing, the statue now felt hot in his pocket.

Chapter 4

The bedroom door had a lock. That was good. Topher closed the door and turned the old-fashioned key. Then he gently placed the statue on the bed, and stood it upright so the cat was facing him.

'Please, Ka, come back.' He knelt on the floor beside her, beside the *statue*, hardly daring to breathe. Was the same frustrating process he'd watched the night before about to begin again? The statue wasn't shining as brightly now, but was that because it was daylight? He got up and closed the blue curtains. Now the room wasn't dark, but it was in shadow and the glow seemed stronger. A golden glow, it glimmered and rippled. He glanced behind him and saw faint circles of light on the wall opposite the statue. He turned back and saw the cat's gleaming eyes.

'Come back. Come back, Ka. Please, come back.'

Brighter now, the ripples ran faster, shimmering, even shuddering. Getting brighter and brighter by the second, the statue – no, *the cat* – was filling out! It – *she* – was growing before his eyes, and yes, stone was becoming fur, starting at the top. One triangular ear then two became velvet soft, then her forehead with the glossy ankh in the centre, then her cheeks.

'Keep coming, Ka.' *Don't stop. Don't go away.* 'Oh!' He clutched the bed as white whiskers sprang from her face, above her eyes and beside her mouth.

Mwow! Her jaws opened to reveal a pink cave edged with sharp white teeth and he held his breath. Surely, surely she couldn't stop coming now?

Ka closed her mouth and looked at him with gleaming amber eyes.

'Topher.' He heard a knock on the door but kept deathly quiet. 'Topher, lunch is ready.'

He concentrated on what was happening in front of him, tried to ignore the noises outside the room. And now tufts of fur were springing from the space between her shoulder blades, her back, her haunches, her hind paws.

Don't stop now.

Ka's tail twitched. Her *furry* tail twitched, and she lifted a *furry* front paw.

Ka was back!

Chapter 5

'Where were you hiding *her*?' Ellie saw Ka on the bed.

'In my pocket.'

She laughed. 'No, really.'

'Look. They're quite big.' Topher turned his pockets inside out.

Ellie laughed again, but didn't continue her interrogation. 'Come on. Mum's got lunch ready, it's pizza, your favourite.'

Reluctant to leave Ka, who had curled up on the bed, Topher slowly followed his friend downstairs.

'We must tell her you've brought Ka,' Ellie continued. 'Duo will be pleased.'

Duo was Ka's son, though when she'd chosen him from the litter, Ellie thought she'd picked a girl kitten. Duo, now a leggy tabby cat, was under the kitchen table hoping someone would drop morsels on the floor for him to gobble up. His eyes, amber like Ka's in daylight, looked green now, shining out from the darkness.

'Duo likes pizza. Ka does as well, doesn't she?' Ellie was chatty – as usual.

'Yup.' Topher didn't feel like speaking, but the Wentworths all talked so much it didn't really matter. No one seemed to notice that he was being quieter than normal, or that he didn't eat much either. He just still didn't feel hungry.

When they'd finished their meal and he and Ellie

were on their way upstairs again, she thrust a list in front of him. 'Now these are all the things we could do. One, there's the Science Museum because we didn't get there last time, two...'

He shook his head. 'Couldn't we just stay in and do stuff on your computer?'

She wrinkled her nose. 'Why?'

Because I want to ask Ka something. But Topher knew he couldn't say that.

'I'm into card games, that's all. Patience. Solo. That sort of stuff.'

'Bor-*ing*! You could do that at home.' Ellie flounced past him into her room but said he could use her computer for half an hour while she finished a good book she was reading. 'But when I've finished it we're going out, right? We could go to Waterlow Park and book a tennis court, or hang out in Highgate.'

She switched on the computer and typed in her password, but then stretched out on her bed, book in hand. Oh. She looked as if she were going to stay there. Could he communicate with Ka with Ellie in the room?

Supposing he'd have to try, Topher went to see Ka. She was still on his bed, all four paws tucked neatly beneath her. He knelt down and whispered in her cut ear, which had healed up fine. 'Where have you been? Where have you been, Ka? Come and tell me.' He picked her up and heard giggles.

'Pussy cat, pussy cat, where have you been? I've been to London to visit the queen!'

23

Russell crawled out from under the bed and rolled across the floor, closely followed by Luke, who ran straight out of the door. Seconds later, Topher heard him informing Ellie that Topher had been reciting nursery rhymes. He heard his friend asking Luke to go away – very rudely – and then Luke pounding downstairs calling, 'I'm telling Mum you said a rude word!'

Luckily Russell quickly decided to follow his brother, but Topher suddenly wished he'd never come to London. He should have stayed at home. He felt sick, and he wanted his own bed and his own computer, and Ellie's brothers were very annoying.

'What do you think, Ka?'

She opened her eyes, her lovely big amber eyes, and began to purr. '*Don't wo...rrrrrrrrrry. Don't wo... rrrrrrrrry.*'

Well, that's what he thought she was saying. 'You'll tell me later where you've been?'

'*Lat...errrrrrrrrr. Lat...errrrrrrrrr.*' She closed her eyes, curled herself into a ball, wrapped her tail around her face and went back to sleep. Topher rested his cheek on the soft cushion of her fur and sniffed, but there was no hint of anything whiffy today. Good! But where had she been? He longed to know.

It wasn't till later that night that he got another chance to ask her. Ellie wanted to stay up and watch something on TV with her parents. The boys were asleep. Topher yawned and said he was going to bed, but when he got upstairs he crept into Ellie's dark room to see if her computer was still on. When he moved the mouse the screen lit up. Yes! She'd forgotten to log off.

He was about to go into his room and fetch Ka when he saw her framed in the doorway. A silhouette against the landing light, she was standing with her tail upright and quivering.

'Come on.' Slowly Topher sat on the chair in front of the computer screen and waited. There was no point in hurrying Ka, or bossing her around. So he just sat, hands on the desk in front of him, hoping she'd come into the room and jump on his knee. Then from the corner of his eye he saw her set out towards him and stop by the side of his chair. He couldn't resist tapping his knee. And she sprang onto it.

'Ouch! Just settle down, will you?' Her claws dug into him, pulling at his jeans and pricking his skin. But after a couple of circuits Ka sat still, claws retracted, facing the screen.

Topher stayed quiet, not daring to move. Ka was upright and alert, not settled.

He peered between her triangular ears at the keyboard and the screen, which glowed in the darkness. 'Where did you go?' he whispered. 'Where did you go, Ka?'

He saw her raise her left paw. Reach out. Hover. Press. *C* appeared on the screen. What next? He held his breath as she moved her paw across the keyboard. *A*. She lifted her right paw and reached for the top of the keyboard. *P* and another *P*.

25

Then – 'Ouch!' – her claws dug in as they both heard someone thumping upstairs.

'I *really* want to know.'

She pressed the keyboard again but he didn't see which letters because Ellie burst into the room. Hands grasped his shoulders. 'Liar! I thought you were going to bed.'

Ka streaked across the room and out of the door.

Ellie stared at the screen.

CAPP . . . ELLIS

'What's that all about?' she asked.

The exact same question was in Topher's head.

Chapter 6

Topher felt ill. Aching in all his joints and as if he was going to be sick. Where was Ka? He lay in the dark, wondering where she'd gone. He hadn't seen her since she'd shot out of Ellie's room earlier – and he needed her. His head was throbbing. He felt hot even without the duvet that he'd kicked onto the floor. Then he suddenly felt shivery cold so he picked up the duvet again, but still couldn't get warm. He needed Ka's soft fur against his skin. He wanted her close to help him get to sleep.

Everyone else was sleeping now. He'd heard foot-steps and doors closing and hushed voices as Mr and Mrs Wentworth went to bed in their room below his. He'd heard the house settling down for the night, floorboards creaking and pipes wheezing but at last growing silent. Now there was just a low hum, something electrical, the fridge perhaps, soothing really. Like a purr, but not a purr. *Ka, where are you?*

CAPPELLIS.

The word on the screen seemed to float in front of him. Was that a place in Italy? It sounded Italian. He tried spelling it out over and over again instead of counting sheep. 'C, A, double P, E, double L, I, S. C, A, double P, E, double L, I, S. C, A, double P...'

But sleep wouldn't come. Not till he found Ka.

'K...' The word wouldn't leave his throat. He was so thirsty. That was why. He reached for a glass of water and it flew away.

'*Water.*' His own voice woke him up. So he must have fallen asleep. Water. He switched on the light. No statue. That was always the first thing he looked for. So Ka was still here, in the house somewhere, unless she'd got out through Duo's cat flap.

Topher got out of bed. 'Glass. Water.' He reminded himself out loud what he wanted and made his way to the door. 'Bathroom.' It was downstairs. Somehow he found it, but everything seemed to be floating. Whirling around him. Bath. Loo. Basin. Going round and round. He tried to grab hold of a tap as the basin passed his nose. He missed and found himself falling through the air into darkness...

'Oh, my God! Darling, come here!' A shout woke him, but Topher didn't want to wake and kept his eyes shut.

'Topher, can you hear me?' A man's voice. 'Cover him, sweetheart. Keep him warm.'

Feet near his face. People rushing. Hands touching.

'Topher, speak to me.' Someone shook his arm and he opened his eyes to see black and white tiles. Where was he? Voices. Too loud. He closed his eyes again.

'He's hot.'

'Take his temperature.'

'Oh my God. Forty.'

'Get the doctor. No, an ambulance. Ring nine-nine-nine.'

'Get him back to bed.'

'No, don't move him.'

'Cover him up.'

'No, he's too hot.'

'What's the matter with Topher?' A voice he knew well. Ellie's. 'Mum! Dad! Why's Topher on the floor?'

'Go back to bed, darling.'

'No! Topher. Topher!' Ellie's voice close. Very close. In his ear. He could feel her breath. 'Look what I found. Here. Feel.' Something cold by his hand. 'It's your statue, Topher. Your statue of Ka. I just found it in my room.'

'Out of the way, young lady.'

'Let the paramedics get to him.'

Things on his chest.

Things in his mouth.

Things moving him.

Things lifting him.

Things taking him down, down, down.

Cold night air.

Blue lights flashing.

Engines roaring.

Sirens blaring.

And just before the ambulance doors closed, Topher caught sight of a bird hovering in the night sky, a bird with a heart-shaped face and ghost-like wings.

But he didn't see the bird following the ambulance as it careered through the streets of north London, taking him to the nearest hospital. He didn't see its round eyes watching every stop and start, every turn and swerve.

He didn't see wings the colour of clotted cream beat the night air.

And when nurses in blue uniforms slipped Topher between crisp white sheets, he didn't see the bird watching and waiting on a windowsill.

Chapter 7

Topher didn't know where he was. Drifting in and out of consciousness, strange sounds and pictures changed places in his head. One moment he was in a dark tunnel with the sound of rushing water in his ears. Next he was in bed at home and his mum was looking down at him. His mum, not Molly, her long fair hair floating round her face and tickling his. One moment Ka was rubbing her cheek against his, purring loudly. Next he was back in the tunnel staring at a bright white light and wondering if he were dying. Isn't that what people said you see – a tunnel with a light at the end – when you were leaving this life to enter another one?

Wired to humming, bleeping machines, Topher lay still, unaware of the drugs dripping into him, or the zig-zag patterns racing across computer screens above his bed. He didn't see the uniformed figures checking the machinery, or leaning over his sleeping body. He didn't see the peaks of the zig-zags leaping higher as his temperature soared and he hovered between life and death.

Gradually, as the sky outside the window turned pink and grey like the pigeons on the rooftops, the bleep-bleeps slowed, the pace of the zig-zags steadied, the peaks flattened and Topher opened his eyes. Modern medicine was rushing to his aid. Antibiotics were working.

'Hello.' His dad and Molly were beside the bed.

So was the statue of Ka. His dad saw him staring at it and looked as if he was going to say something, but Molly spoke, 'We'll take care of Ka, Topher. You just get better.'

'But you can't.' His voice was a whisper and hurt his throat. 'She's – gone.'

'She'll come back. She always does.'

She'll come back. She'll come back. She'll come back. He drifted off again with the words in his head. *She'll come back.*

But when he woke and glanced to one side all he could see was the statue. *She'll come back.* But she hadn't.

So I must go and find her. He nearly said the words out loud, when a nurse came in. As she removed a contraption from his hand, she commented on the stone cat. 'We don't usually allow things from outside in intensive care, but the lady who came in with you seemed to think it might help.'

He nodded. That must have been Mrs Wentworth but he bet it was Ellie's idea.

'So we sterilised it and hoped for the best.'

When the nurse had gone Topher touched the statue. Cold. Icy cold. So Ka was far away. Hope for the best. That wasn't enough.

I must go and find her.

But how? As he lay back against the pillows, the sounds of the busy hospital filled his ears. Trolleys rolling. Metal clanging. Voices murmuring. Bleeps

32

bleeping. Buzzers buzzing. Hospital smells drifted up his nose; disinfectant and food like school dinners. Through the half-open door he saw a trolley full of plates in the corridor outside and hoped it wouldn't come in. A breeze sidled into his room from the open window and so did traffic noises: a constant rumble, only broken by the wail of sirens or a screech of brakes.

He guessed he was high up as he could see the tops of buildings and a strip of dull, blue sky. Lower down, a few black shapes were circling – rooks or pigeons, he guessed, London birds. The sky darkened. It must be late evening, he thought, but he couldn't see any stars. You never could in London.

I must go and find Ka.

'Do you want the light on?' A nurse looked in.

He shook his head. There were enough lights outside, windows in high rises and flashing adverts.

'You're right. Probably best to get some more sleep.' The nurse was still there. 'Do you want me to lower your back rest?'

Topher nodded, though now he just wanted her to go away, for something had caught his eye. Perched on the ledge outside, a bird with a white heart-shaped face was looking in through the glass.

'Goodnight. Ring if you want anything.' The nurse showed him a bell push attached to the bed and left.

As soon as he was sure she'd gone, Topher got out of bed and shakily made his way to the window where he grasped the sill.

Tee-whit. A small sharp screech made him grasp the sill in surprise.

But he knew what was happening, for it had happened before.

And he knew what he must do.

'I'm coming.'

Using a chair as a step, he climbed onto the windowsill and suddenly the bird in front of him grew. But it hadn't. He knew that too. He had shrunk, though he didn't feel any shrinking sensation. He didn't feel himself folding up like a telescope, or anything like that. But he had become tiny, so the bird towered over him. Round eyes were looking down on him. His eyes were level with the middle of the bird's feathery legs. Looking down, he saw scaly clawed feet.

Tee-whit. It jumped so that it was sideways on and lowered the wing nearest him. Cream-gold feathers opened like a fan.

Tee-whit. Get on – Topher knew that's what the bird meant.

He climbed up, grasping the shiny feathers with his hands, gripping hard so the barbules beneath sprang apart. He held firm as he climbed higher and higher. Then, when he was about half-way up, the bird lifted its wing.

Tee-whit. Let go.

Topher did and immediately felt himself rolling onto the softer feathers of the bird's back. As he struggled into a sitting position astride the bird, he felt the whoosh of wings either side of him, a surge of energy beneath him, and then air was forcing back his hair and pyjama jacket as the bird took to the night sky. With amazing speed it flew higher and higher till London looked like Legoland beneath him; the River Thames a thread looping its way down to the sea.

'I'm coming, Ka. I'm coming.' For he was sure of it, he was off again, time travelling, to wherever and *when*ever Ka was waiting.

Soon he could see stars, huge stars, for he was among them. Shooting stars with fiery tails overtook him. Smouldering meteors just missed him. And there were stars for as far as he could see, huge balls of fire close to him, tiny sparks in the distance. Trillions and zillions of stars dazzled him with their brilliance so he had to close his eyes, and when he opened them the wind had dropped. He was in space, in a vacuum, travelling through times and dimensions he couldn't name, in a silence so pure he could hear his own heart pumping. And there was Earth, like a giant globe, a sphere that was growing rapidly bigger, so he must be coming in to land. He recognised Europe and Asia and the snowy Arctic. Where was he going this time? Now he could feel the bird braking beneath him, see its wings on either side pulling back, feel the force of the wind scraping back his own hair – and there was the River Thames below him again. He'd recognise those snaky curves anywhere. Any *when*. London. He spotted the dome of St Paul's and wondered what person, in what century, he was going to be this time. Then he had to grip on tight, his arms round the bird's neck as it descended with great speed.

Tee whit. Get off.

It tipped him onto the cobbles and Topher immediately knew he was in the past. For a few seconds, as the bird flew off, he was aware of where he had come from. Then, as a disgusting smell filled his nose and made him gasp, all memory of his life as Topher Hope faded.

He was Topher Rowley, an orphan on the run...

Chapter 8

'Gotcha!'

But he hadn't. Topher pulled free and dived under the whelk stall just in time.

'Come out, boy!' Pale piggy eyes glared at him and a huge hairy hand made a grab.

But Topher was off. On hands and knees, fast as a ferret he scrabbled beneath the row of stalls, slipping and sliding on wet cobbles and bits of chopped fish, hoping none of the stallholders would shop him. Go back to the workhouse? Never. Back to oakum picking and near starvation? Never. Back to beatings and stone-breaking? Never never *never*.

'Very good herring! Very good herring!'

Good? They smelled disgusting, or something did. Topher tried not to breathe through his nose as he came to the end of the row.

'*Aaagh!*' A cry and a crash. Sounded like someone had slipped. The master, he hoped. What now? He peered out at spats and leather boots and some bare feet. Whose? That were the question. Lifting the cloth covering the stall, he saw the skimpy skirt of a servant girl buying fish, the wider skirt of a well-built woman – looked like a cook – and a couple of older coves. But not Mr Godfrey. Not the master. Well, both coves had mufflers wrapped around their faces, so it was hard to tell, but – he checked again – neither of them had spats on their feet like the master's. Phew! He crawled out and got to his feet.

Don't run, Topher told himself. *Saunter.* So he did, or tried to. But there were a lot of folks coming the other way, crowds of them, in the devil of a hurry. It was hard to keep on his feet, let alone look casual. *Careful does it. Don't slip*, he tried to think as he threaded his way through buckets of wriggling eels and crates of cockles and whelks. He'd left in a hurry, that was the trouble. He'd just seen the open door at the workhouse and run, so he didn't have a plan. But head for the river, he thought that's what he should do.

'You, boy, what yer doing?' A stallholder waved a filleting knife.

'See his shaved head and his shirt,' said another. 'He's escaped from the workhouse.'

'I'm looking for my da.' *If only.* Topher pulled the edges of his jacket together to hide the blue and grey stripes.

'Where's he then?'

Six feet under. Pauper's grave. Don't think about it. Get down to the docks and get some work loading boats. Get aboard if you can. Stow away. Sail off to a foreign land.

That was his plan, but getting to the river was proving harder than he'd thought. Upper Thames Street. That's where he was heading. It ran alongside the river. But now he was hardly moving. There were too many coves coming the other way, holding him back. A lot of Jack Tars among them coming from their boats. Pushing and shoving. And not just folk. There were horses too, some pulling carriages and hansom cabs. Topher tried to weave his way through, against the surge, but now there was hardly any space between vehicles. Must be careful. A cove copped it last week. Squashed between two carts.

'Steady on!' Someone nearly knocked him off his feet.

'Blimey riley!' Topher staggered backwards. It weren't just the folk pushing. It was the stink, wet like a smelly hand in your face. No wonder folks were all muffled up.

'Out the way, glock!' A toff on horseback raised his whip.

'Read all about it!' A newspaper seller was yelling about his wares, but stopped when he was squeezed upward by the surging crowd. Topher suddenly felt his own feet leave the ground. Felt himself being carried backwards till he managed to grab hold of a crate and pull himself sideways into a doorway. He saw the newspaper cove had taken refuge there too.

'Read all about it! Read all about the Great Stink! Her majesty turned back from pleasure cruise! Houses of Parliament vacated!'

The Thames stinking. What sort of news was that? It always stank. No wonder, with all the folks' doodahs going into it and all the blood and dog doodahs from the leather works, and the dyes and stuff from the factories. Like bad eggs and privies mixed together, it were. Eye stinging. And maybe it were worse today. That would be the hot weather. So *that's* why everyone was running away from the river, but Topher had to go towards it. Had to get as far from the workhouse as he could. Get caught now and it would be the whipping post.

So which way? Crouched behind the paper seller, Topher looked left and right before catching sight of a cove in the doorway of the pawnbroker's opposite. Only the man's back was visible, but it looked familiar and he was talking to a peeler. Nod, nod, nod went the familiar head with its stringy yellow hair. Nod, nod, nod went the peeler's domed helmet and Topher spotted the truncheon hanging from his leather belt. Then, just as the paper seller picked up his bag and moved away, Mr Godfrey, the master – the familiar head was his – turned and looked straight at Topher with his pale pig-eyes. Then he turned to the peeler, who blew hard on his whistle. And Topher froze.

Run was in his head. *The river. Must get to the river.* But the crowds were still pushing in the opposite direction and his feet couldn't move. Then they could. He forced them forward. *Faster. Faster.* But they couldn't go faster, not against the tide of folk forcing him the other way. *Into an alley and out the other side.* That was his plan and he found one, but then he couldn't get out of it. Couldn't get back onto the street.

There were just as many folk in this street, and horses and carriages and carts, all fighting their way from the river. Only one good thing, no one seemed to be taking any notice of peelers or workhouse masters or workhouse boys or anything. Where was Mr Godfrey?

Where was the peeler? No sign. Good. Right. *One two three – go!* Forcing himself forward, Topher penetrated the tide of folk, weaving between them like a shuttle.

'Sorry, missus,' he said, knocking into a lady.

'Stupid boy!' A toff in a top hat steered her away.

Now Topher was gasping. The stink was terrible and he had nothing to cover his face with. It weren't just a smell. The air was thick. He could *taste* the filth.

Keep going. Keep going.

Trying to keep his mouth shut, he kept going and finally the crowd started to thin out. It became easier to move, and he came to a junction. He was back at Upper Thames Street, but now it was nearly empty. No sign of the master or the peeler. No wonder. Folk with any sense had all got away from here – and the stench – as fast as they could.

Wiping his mouth on his jacket sleeve, Topher paused to gather his thoughts. He could see warehouses on the other side of the road and an alley running between two of them. Through this gap he spotted masts and sails and funnels, boats and ships of all kinds. Escape! If only he could get onto one of them.

But now the stink was like a *thing* pushing him back with a wet, smelly, giant hand. He could feel it on his face. But he had to go forward. It was his only chance. So, bent double, holding his nose shut, he crossed the street and staggered along the alley. And there was the river, if you could call something solid a river. Nothing moved. The boats and ships couldn't budge. They were stuck. Nothing was moving except the rats and flies feeding off the filthy sludge that bubbled and popped like a hellish brown stew. The River Thames was a huge cesspit.

In the distance a plume of smoke puffed into the sky, most like from a steam train leaving Fenchurch Station. Crowded with folk fleeing the city probably. *What now?*

As Topher wished he could leave London too, he felt violent hands grip his shoulder.

Chapter 9

Was it the master, Mr Godfrey?

As Topher glanced over his shoulder he saw a face as red as a ham, bristling with black whiskers. Not Mr Godfrey, but this cove clearly meant no good, and his grip on Topher tightened. So, quick as a lizard discarding its tail, Topher pulled his arms out of the sleeves, leaving his jacket behind. Glad for once the jacket was far too big for him, Topher dodged to the left, then left again, and then turned right, back into the alley and down it. Fast as one of the newfangled trains he went, arms and legs going like pistons. Didn't know if he was being chased or not. Didn't stop to find out. And when he got to the end of the alley he kept running, over the road, near empty now, thank the Lord, then left and right again to confuse the cove if he were still following. Till he had to stop, bent double. Exhausted, gulping for breath, he hated sucking in the filthy stench.

Only then did Topher look.

No one behind, not chasing him anyhow. Nor to the left or right. Nor ahead. There were a few folk about but not the one who now had his jacket. That must have been all the thieving cove wanted.

He heard a cry: 'Pretty ribbons! Penny a roll!' So he must be near St Paul's where the drapers had their stalls round the edges of the churchyard. Yes, looking up he saw the dome of the church, the highest building around, with a cross on top, even higher, shining in the sunlight. This was the market where Ma used to buy her thread and stuff. But best not to think of Ma or Da. Best think where to hide. He was more noticeable now without his jacket covering his striped workhouse shirt.

And where could he get some grub? His stomach was aching. Would one of the stallholders help him out for old time's sake? His ma had been a good customer once, though she went from one to the other trying to strike a bargain. Nah! Most of them had gone home, and he'd tried them all before. Said he'd do any work: take messages, look out for tea leaves, fetch and carry, mind the stall. Anything. But they'd all turned him down and they'd dob him to the peelers or the master most like, soon as look at him. Then, quicker than you could say horse droppings, he'd be back in the workhouse.

The workhouse. The memory was enough to sharpen his wits. The gruel. The treadmill. The beatings. Mr Godfrey, that's who he should be looking out for. Setting off again, but slower so as not to draw attention to himself, Topher walked past the posh folks' graves with their fancy headstones. In the shadow of the huge building he felt the lack of his coat. He'd feel the need of it more when night came.

Keeping close to the south wall of the church, he made his way to the steps at the front. He climbed to the top of them and got behind one of the stone pillars. From there he could see the maze of streets leading down to the river. So far so good. There was still no sign of anyone looking for him. No sign of the peeler or Mr

Godfrey anyway. But who was that at the bottom of the steps, eyes darting about like a sewer rat?

Snoop. He'd recognise him anywhere. He did look like a rat with his pointed chin and sticking-out whiskers. No hair on his top lip, just these bristles at the sides. Well in with Mr Godfrey, was Snoop. So most like he was doing his dirty work now. He'd started off as one of the lads in the workhouse but soon got a job helping Mr Godfrey, as a reward for snooping on the others.

Topher dodged back behind the pillar. *What now? Hide in the church?* As he thought about it, a small door cut into one of the huge doors opened and through it he saw something shining. Candles, hundreds of them, flickered and gleamed, lighting up golden pillars like huge twists of barley sugar. Then a top-hatted gentleman stepped out and sniffed, looking about before stepping back through the door and snapping it shut. Chance gone. And Snoop was still at the bottom of the steps, talking to another cove now. Best scarper while he weren't looking. Where though? If he went west along the Strand he might be able to pick up a job at Charing Cross. If he had a job they'd have no reason to put him in the workhouse.

Hunger made him slow. By the time he reached the famous crossroads the bells of half a dozen churches were striking noon. There weren't many folk about, only stagecoach drivers on their high seats, their faces muffled. There was the usual jam of coaches waiting to get into the Golden Cross inn. Four hundred a day he'd heard, bringing in folk from all over England. All the

45

coach blinds were tightly closed to try and keep out the stink, but the waiting horses were only adding to it. The cobbles steamed with their doodahs.

A hiring cove, under the statue of a king on a horse, told him there was no call for lads, only chambermaids. 'So better go back to the workhouse, lad. At least you'll get fed there.'

Then Topher came across a boy sweeper who said he'd heard there might be a job going at the zoo in Regent's Park, cleaning out the animal cages. So Topher headed north, across the new Trafalgar Square and into Regent Street.

And it was there that he met the cat.

He'd stopped to cross Argyll Street when it streaked out of a doorway, past a fine lady whose emerald-green crinoline skirt was so wide it nearly covered the pavement. But the lady didn't see the cat. The brim of her bonnet acted like horses' blinkers. Also she held a lace 'kerchief to her nose – no doubt to block the stink that though fainter still hung in the air. She was reading from a poster on the wall to a little girl dressed just like her.

'Listen, Maria. *Signor Cappelli's Learned Cats*. First the cat orchestra will play, then Ka – the cleverest of the company – it says here will draw water out of a well, walk the tightrope and talk in English, Italian and Chinese. That is what we shall see today if Papa can purchase tickets.'

'Purchased, my dear.' A gentleman with glossy black hair and striking triangular side-whiskers appeared in the doorway. He took the lady's arm and Topher noticed the cat beneath her skirt. It was peeping out and looking up at *him*. Round amber eyes looked straight into his. He felt sure of it.

Shhh. Don't tell. Words came into Topher's head.

Then a taller dark-haired man rushed out of the building. Face as white as paper, he had a thin black moustache that curled up at the ends. 'Ka! Ka! Catt-a! Catt-a! Come back-a here! Gentleman, lady, leetle girl? You, boy?' He noticed Topher last. 'Deed-a you see catt-a?' And when they all shook their heads, the man went back inside.

'Papa, was that Signor Cappelli?' the little girl asked.

'I think so, my dear.' The fine gentleman's hand was in his pocket, as if searching for his 'kerchief.

'Do you think he has lost one of the learned cats, Papa?'

'Yes, the cleverest I think.'

Topher noticed the man's white linen kerchief on the ground next to the cat. Next to Ka, the cleverest of the learned cats, who was still hidden under the lady's skirt.

'Excuse me, sir.' As he picked up the 'kerchief he noticed a key-like mark on the cat's forehead.

'Thank you, lad.' The man mopped his brow and looked Topher up and down. 'An honest boy. Good.'

Topher felt him notice the workhouse shirt.

'Do you want work, lad?'

'Yes, but not in the workhouse, sir.'

The man looked thoughtful and took a card from his pocket, then he shook his head and made to put it back again.

'I can read, sir. I learned at Sunday school.' That had been in his old village, where he'd lived before he and his family came to London.

'Clever too?' The man raised a bushy black eyebrow, handing him the card. 'Then bring this to my office tomorrow.'

> Mr Joseph Bazalgette
> Chief Engineer
> Metropolitan Board of Works
> 24 George Street

He'd turned his back and opened the door before Topher could ask where George Street was. But Topher noticed that the man's daughter was looking back at him. He was thinking how bright her blue eyes were, when she winked. At him. *Why?* Her gaze shifted and he followed it to the cat, now peeping out from behind a stone urn. Then she followed her parents inside as Signor Cappelli came out again. 'You want-a earn money?'

Topher nodded vigorously and the man held out a florin. 'Yours, if you find catt-a.'

'It's . . .' But when he looked the cat had gone. Perhaps for the best. The man might withdraw his offer if he saw Ka so near himself. With a florin, Topher could buy food for a week.

'First-a you need-a picture of the catt-a. Come.'

He followed the man inside and into a darkened room, hoping the cat wouldn't vanish completely. The room was filled with fine ladies and gentlemen waiting for the show to begin. All eyes were on the dimly lit stage where the cat orchestra was poised to start playing. A tabby held drumsticks over a drum. A glossy black cat sat on a cushion with a bunch of bells in each of her forepaws. A fluffy ginger sat before a xylophone and a fourth, another tabby, was sitting on a stool with its paws over the keyboard of a pianola. All were very still. *Amazing!*

'Hurry, boy. Thees-a way.' Mr Cappelli hustled him along the side of the room, through a door beside the stage, into the wings. 'Come.' He yanked Topher's arm and pulled him into a side room, but not before he had spotted the wire around the drummer cat's paws.

The showman thrust a daguerreotype of the missing cat in front of Topher.

'See the mark – like a key – on her head? That's how you will know her. *Yes?*' His Italian accent had suddenly disappeared.

'Yes.' Topher had noticed that same mark beneath a lady's emerald satin skirt just minutes ago. But now he was distracted by something else – bottles of green liquid marked CHLOROFORM and coils of fine wire like that he'd seen around the tabby's paws. So *that* was how Cappelli got the cats to do what he wanted. He drugged them.

'So, when you find the cat you clip this onto its collar.' The man, the *trickster*, put a lead in Topher's hand. Then he led him back into the passage, where he opened another door to the street outside. 'Pronto. For a

49

florin.' He closed the door and went back inside leaving Topher in a narrow alley, where a dead cat, another tabby, lay stiff on the cobbles near the wall. It looked as if Mr Cappelli sometimes gave a cat too much chloroform.

He heard the man's voice from inside. 'Ladies and gentlemen-a, prepar-a yourself for a magical, miaow-arvellous mew-usical extravaganza, a feline ...'

'Fraud,' said Topher, and he wished he wasn't so desperate to eat.

Chapter 10

If only he weren't so hungry.

Where was the cat? There was *a* cat sitting on the top step of the house opposite. But it was white with black patches and in danger of toppling off the step while trying to lick its rear end. Ah, there it went roly-poly, roly-poly, right to the bottom. *Not* a learned cat.

Topher looked again at the likeness Signor Cappelli had given him. The cat's fur was golden with lines and flecks of white and black – unusual, but not as unusual as the key-like mark on her forehead. From the front he would recognise her easily – if he ever saw her again.

There were lots of places for a cat to hide, and this cat obviously didn't want to be caught. He knew that now, and he knew why. She could have climbed one of the trees lining the road further up. She could be hiding in the shrubbery of any of the gardens nearby. The phrase *Looking for a needle in a haystack* came into Topher's head. This part of London wasn't a maze of streets like it was further south nearer the river. The streets here were wider, the big white houses weren't crammed together and the doors had shiny brass knockers, but there were still plenty of places for a cat to hide.

Ka had been a prisoner of Cappelli.

Like me in the workhouse.

But she had escaped.

Just like me. So do I really want to catch her and take her back? No, but...

Hunger gnawed at his stomach, making him feel sick. *Sorry, cat, but I need food.*

So which way had she gone?

'Beep! Beep!'

The strange cry came from a cats' meat man. There he was in his blood-stained shirt and leather jerkin, coming into the street, pushing his barrow. Like the Pied Piper he were, but with cats not rats. There were near a dozen of the creatures following him. Most like Ka would be with them. She'd know a good thing when she saw it.

'Ha'penny snack or a threepenny feast!' called the man.

Blimey riley. Threepenny feast. Rich folk spent more on their cats than his ma had to feed the whole family.

'Gerroff, you tea leaf!' The cove hit out at a ginger tom. 'Beep! Beep! Come and buy!'

As the man got closer Topher felt his mouth watering. It was most likely horse meat and some of it looked a bit grey but it would cook up all right. Wash it in vinegar. That's what his ma did. But he must concentrate on finding the cat. A florin would buy him even more grub.

A dozen cats were all over the pushcart now and the meat man was getting shirty. 'Geroff!' He hit out in all directions at cats and flies, only just missing a customer.

'Want a hand, mister?' He might earn himself a dinner this way.

'Nah, get lost, yer little tea leaf.'

'I'm no tea leaf. I could keep the flies off.'

But the man raised his fist. 'Scarper, I said!'

So scarper Topher did, once he'd checked again that Ka wasn't there amongst the hungry cats.

Rounding a bend, he found himself in a really posh road. Gentry lived here for sure. Their fancy white houses curved round in a half-circle like an enormous iced cake. *Cake!* Topher wished he could stop thinking of food. Horse-drawn carriages waited outside some of the doors. Bored drivers twitched their whips to keep away the flies.

So where were the cats? There was a long-eared dog sleeping under one of the pillared porches, but he couldn't see any cats at all, not a single one. Topher was thinking that they must all be inside sleeping on velvet cushions, when he noticed black railings on the other side of the road and grass beyond. Then he caught a glimpse of a brightly coloured bird and heard it squawk. *The zoo!* He must have reached Regent's Park. Now he remembered the job cleaning cages he'd heard about from that sweeper.

Earn an honest living. That would be better than handing the cat back to Cappelli.

Go free, cat! Take your chance like me!

And if he didn't get the job at the zoo, there was that offer from Mr Bazalgette. That was tomorrow though, and he was hungry today. So where were the gates to the zoo? Topher looked left and right but couldn't see any. They must be round the other side then. But which side, left or right? If he'd had a coin he'd have tossed it to help him decide. Then he saw a peeler coming down the street from the right swinging his truncheon. Not that way then. Not left neither. That red-brick building in the distance looked like a workhouse – The Marylebone, he'd heard about that. *So turn round and go back the way you came. Sharpish. But don't run*, he warned himself. *Not till you're out of sight of the peeler.*

He was about half-way down Regent Street when he saw a cat. *The* cat, sitting on a gatepost outside a grand house. He knew her even before he saw her face. There was something about the way she held herself. He expected her to jump and run away as soon as she saw him, but she didn't. It was as if she was waiting for him. *Now what?* he thought as he reached the gateway.

Her round amber eyes looked straight into his. Her mouth opened. 'Hide.'

Had she really spoken? Now he saw the cats' meat man by the tradesman's entrance at the side of the house. '*Hide.*'

The cat had definitely spoken. Topher did what she told him and stepped behind the gatepost. Then he saw the cove go inside the house, leaving his barrow behind. And suddenly the cat sprang down, raced along the drive and into a shrubbery. For a few seconds he couldn't see her. Then there she was on the barrow. Then she was racing up the drive towards him, a skewer of meat between her jaws.

Mi-ew. Take it. She was looking up at him.

Five chunks of juicy, red meat. A threepenny feast.

'But...' How could he roast it? What if the peeler saw him with it? What if the cats' meat man gave chase?

Mi-ew. Take it. She looked into his eyes.

So he took it.

Ka started running down the street back towards Charing Cross. And Topher followed as fast as he could. Luckily there weren't many folk about, he didn't see any peelers and eventually she slowed down. Now some of the roads looked familiar. He thought they were quite near where he used to live in Broad Street. And for a while the cat sauntered, tail quivering like a flame.

A cove with a red 'kerchief around his neck stopped to speak to her. 'Hello, catito . . . '

But that was all Topher understood, for the cove spoke in a foreign tongue. He guessed they were now in Soho where he used to deliver shoes for his pa. If only he could see a roast-chestnut seller or a hot-potato man. *Go halves, mister?* He rehearsed what he'd say in his head if he saw someone who could cook the meat for him. But summer wasn't the season for baked potatoes or roast chestnuts, and it was too early in the day to find a night watchman with a brazier.

SSSSSsssssss! Suddenly the cat was hissing. Fur bristling, back arched, she was glaring at someone behind him. Warning him. But before Topher could run or turn to see, the someone had grabbed his arm.

'Toffee.'

The voice was friendly but the knife in his side wasn't.

'Walk on nice and slow, like, if you don't want to feel Slim in your side.'

Chapter 11

Only one person called him Toffee. Back in the workhouse Snoop told everyone he thought Topher was a bit of a toff, just because he could read and write.

'I said walk.' Snoop's rat face was too close.

SSSSsssss! Ka leaped at the cove's leg.

'Scat, cat!' He kicked her away.

'*RRRrrrun!*' She stood her ground, just clear of Snoop's foot, begging Topher to leave.

But Snoop's knife was jabbing into him. 'You remember Slim, don't you, Toffee? Could cut a cat's throat – or yours.'

'*RRRrrrun!*' Ka looked up into Topher's eyes – and he saw a tiny medallion hanging from her neck.

And so did Snoop. 'A toff's cat, eh? Nice reward for the return of *them*!' Sliding his knife into one of his boots, he grabbed the skewer of meat and held it at arm's length. 'Come here, puss. Puss, puss, puss.' Then, 'Ow!' His newly bleeding hand shot to his mouth.

And Ka was running up the road holding the skewer.

Topher ran too, but not fast enough. Snoop had let go of him briefly but soon had hold of his arm again, the knife in his bleeding hand. It was back to Mr Godfrey, Topher thought...

'Walk on all natural like,' Snoop murmured, sounding less friendly than before. 'And keep beside me. Go on. Walk.'

What could he do? One or two folks stared at them from doorways, but most took no notice. They wouldn't understand if he did ask them for help. Most likely they wouldn't care if they did, not even if he said he was being forced back to the workhouse.

'Foreigners.' Snoop spat on the ground. 'Taking over they are. Soho, it's not like merry England any more. No wonder they calls this Greek Street.'

The workhouse seemed to be where they were heading. The smell of the river was getting stronger. Eye-watering it was and Snoop noticed, though he guessed at the wrong reason for Topher's tears.

'No need to blub, Toffee. I ain't taking you back to Mr Godfrey, if that's what you're thinking. We're not going back to the workhouse. Oh, no. I've moved on, I have. Got better prospects now and so have you, Toffee, if you keeps yer nose clean. See, stick by Snoop and you'll be all right. Go on. Hurry up. Get a move on.'

Not the workhouse! So where was Snoop taking him?

'Not the barracks neither.' Snoop pointed ahead to a castle-like building, where soldiers in red uniforms guarded the entrance. 'Don't think you want to be cannon fodder, do yer, Toffee?'

Snoop didn't sound like the nasty cove he'd been in the workhouse, and Topher felt a little surge of hope. Perhaps Snoop had had a change of heart? Perhaps he was taking him somewhere he could earn an honest living? Perhaps this was his lucky day?

'What are these prospects, Snoop?'

But Snoop didn't answer, and doubts set in. Three job offers in one day – wasn't that a bit too good to be true? And if Snoop meant well, why was he taking him there at knife-point? They reached Trafalgar Square where a couple of coves were straining their necks to look at the statue on top of the tallest plinth.

'Lord Nelson,' said Snoop. 'But you don't want to join the navy neither, do yer, Toffee? Not now. Though it were better when the admiral was in charge. Looked after his men did Lord Nelson. Lost some, but not as many as the enemy. Foreigners, they're not so good at fighting as us Brits.'

He steered Topher across the square and into Charing Cross, which was still clogged up with stagecoaches waiting to unload passengers at the Golden Cross. Topher wondered if he should try and make a break for it here. But where would he go?

'Stop daydreaming, Toffee.' Snoop pointed to a side street. 'We need to get over there into Cockspur, then down towards Saint Giles. Go on. Get a move on. A squirt like you can squeeze between them two hansom cabs.'

The houses in the next street looked as if they'd seen better days. Well, most of them did. One or two had white-scrubbed steps and painted doors with shiny brass doorknobs, but most of them had peeling paint and broken windows.

'Gentry moved west,' said Snoop. 'So we moved in. Can't let good property go to waste, can we?'

He didn't say who 'we' were, but Topher saw him nod at an upstairs window of one of the houses about half-way down the street. He saw faces pressed against the panes.

'This is where your new life begins,' Snoop told him as the door to the house opened.

At the top of some steps stood a red-faced fellow, with his hands behind his back. Topher was just thinking that he'd seen those black bristles before when the fellow gave out a wheezy laugh.

'Welcome to the Rookery, lad. So called cos we live as close as rooks in trees. But I'm sure you'll find it cosier than the spike. Looking for this, are you?' With a flourish he extended a huge arm and there, dangling from the cove's hairy fingers, was Topher's own tweed jacket.

Chapter 12

He'd come to a den of tea leaves.

'And you'll make a very good one,' said the red-faced cove as he led the way upstairs. 'You're quick, you are. Nifty. A proper little escapologist.'

'Mr Wiggins knows talent when he sees it,' said Snoop bringing up the rear. 'Mind you, I were surprised when Mr Wiggins told me it was your coat, Toffee.'

As Topher felt Snoop's knife in his back again he knew he was trapped between the devil and the deep blue sea. Mr Wiggins and Snoop might look very different from each other; one old, one young, one solid as a boulder, the other skinny as an eel, but they were both lowlife.

'Ouch!' cried what looked like a heap of rags in a stairwell, as they trampled on him. 'Mind your plates of meat!'

There were more young coves sleeping on the stairs, Topher noted, and more on the landing. All the rooms were full of folk, Snoop said, and this was the overflow. Then Mr Wiggins half opened a door and stuck his head inside.

'A new apprentice, Mr Squittle, name of Topher – or Toffee as he's known, on account of his being a bit of a toff. Snoop here says the lad can read and write.'

'Let's see him then.' The voice that answered was old and scratchy, but when Topher followed Mr Wiggins inside, he couldn't see who it belonged to. There was a window at one end of the room, the window he'd seen from the street, but it was so dirty it didn't let in much light. Now the heads that had been pressed to the panes all turned to look at him, but he couldn't see their faces.

'Let's see what he can do then.' The scratchy voice came from another part of the room, and as Topher's eyes got used to the gloom, he made out the top half of a man with a bald head sitting in a low chair by an empty fireplace. Was he in charge? The others seemed to act as if he were, even Mr Wiggins.

'He might need learning, Mr Squittle,' said Snoop, still very close.

'Can he pick a pocket?'

'Hasn't been brought up to it, Mr Squittle.'

'Better learn him then.'

'Right, lads, who's gonna show the new cove how to pick a pocket?' Mr Wiggins, who towered over everyone else, stood in the middle of the room and looked around. So did Topher. As well as the group by the window, he saw even more bodies asleep on the floor.

A titchy cove with a mouth as wide as his face sprang from somewhere and crouched by Mr Wiggins' feet.

'All right, Froggy,' he laughed. 'You'll do.'

'I'll be your dupe, right,' said Mr Wiggins. 'I'm a fine gentleman. Now pass me a shilling someone. Come on. Wake up!'

Someone handed him a silver coin and he bit it. 'Good one this.' He put it in the side pocket of his checked breeches.

'Now, Froggy, I'll saunter up the road, so to speak, and you show Toffee here how to get the coin, right?'

The other boys moved back to make a space. Then Mr Wiggins began to walk up the room, chest puffed out as if he were a regular toff in one of the new emporiums. He pretended he was looking in a shop window, then he turned round and patted his pocket. Then he moved off again, coming down the other side of the room. Topher didn't see Froggy go near him, but suddenly there he was on the other side of the room with the coin and a pocket book held high. Fast as lightning. Topher hadn't even seen Froggy's hand go into Mr Wiggins's pockets.

Nor had Mr Wiggins. The first he knew about being robbed was when the others cheered. But he was pleased. 'Nice bit of buzzing, Froggy. Well done, lad. Hope you were watching, Toffee.'

Friendly. That's what he sounded like, but he weren't friendly when he felt Topher trying to pick his pocket. *Bang!* Down came his hand, hard as a stick. Again and again. 'You disappoint me, Toffee. I expected better from the way you slipped out of that jacket. Fast as a ferret you were. You'd better try snowing when we can trust you to go outside.'

Topher soon realised there was a new language to learn here as well. Snowing meant stealing clothes that had been hung on a washing line to dry.

'We all have to earn our keep in this family,' Snoop said later.

Family? It wasn't like any family Topher remembered. *Honesty is the best policy*, that's what his ma and pa had always said. They earned every penny they had. Ma by sewing shirts, Pa by making shoes night and day. But even that didn't bring in enough money to stop them going hungry, and Pa didn't spend their money on grog like Mr Squittle seemed to. Maybe that's why he appeared to sleep most of the time. But the food here looked good. Topher could hardly believe it when Mr Wiggins brought in a tray of meat pies and Mr Squittle had handed them out – to most of the boys, but not all.

'Not you,' he said to one. 'You haven't earned your keep, you haven't.' He'd made the lad watch the others eating.

Topher got a closer look at Mr Squittle at the end of the day, when someone lit the fire. The man felt the cold it seemed, even in June. Bundled in a chair, half covered by a plaid rug, his grizzled head and blue-veined nose looked too big for the rest of his body.

'Lost his legs at Balaclava, he did, fighting for queen and country,' said Snoop. 'Carried to the field hospital by Army here, nursed back to health by the famous Lady with the Lamp herself. Then what?'

'They threw him in the spike,' growled Army McAvoy, a curly-haired cove, never far from Mr Squittle's side. He was the only one who called him Squittle without the 'mister'.

'And that's where you'll be again, Toffee,' said Snoop, 'if you don't learn how to bring back three shillings a day. But don't worry. In the meantime you can read us a story like you did in the spike. To earn that meat pie you've eaten. What's this one?' He held up a book.

'*Oliver Twist* by Charles Dickens.'

Snoop tossed it aside. 'We don't want to hear little Oliver weeping and wailing, do we? But you could learn a lesson from him, Toffee. Don't ever think of snitching. Don't go singing to the peelers or you'll get nobbled good and proper.' He handed Topher another book.

'*Jack Sheppard.*'

'*Jack Sheppard*, you coves!'

At Snoop's shout the others moved nearly as fast as they had when Mr Wiggins said 'pies'.

They gathered round Topher and he began reading.

Soon the room was silent except for Topher's voice, telling them about the dashing highway robber. They listened avidly, and he knew that in their minds they were all out on the highway, mounted on their trusty steeds, trigger fingers poised – till it grew dark and Mr Squittle banged his crutch on the floor.

Mr Wiggins heaved himself to his feet. 'Come on, lads. It's time for the night shift to go and do a bit of Jack Shepparding.' Half a dozen coves made their way to the door. Others bedded down on various heaps and bundles on the floor.

'And there's a billet for you, Toffee.' Snoop pointed to a heap of sacks near the window. 'Go on. Lie down. You've got a busy day tomorrow.'

It was good to rest, but as he lay in the darkness Topher couldn't help worrying. The food was good, but what he was learning here was wrong. If he got caught stealing he'd be sent to prison, or worse. Going over his eventful day he remembered the card in his pocket and Mr Bazalgette's words. 'Come to my office in the morning.' But how could he? How could he get out of here? He was trapped, and if he didn't do what he was told he'd suffer for it. The rule was clear. If you pleased Mr Squittle you got pies. If you didn't you suffered. There were plenty ready to carry out the legless man's orders. His arm throbbed where Mr Wiggins had walloped it and he'd seen Army McAvoy hit out at another lad when Mr Squittle had given him the nod.

From time to time something scurried over his face. He wished the amazing cat he'd met earlier that day were here. She'd make short work of mice or cockroaches. Once he thought he heard her mewing outside, but when he kneeled up and looked through the window, he couldn't see a thing. She really was a clever cat. She'd even spoken to him. She'd tried to help him.

Had Signor Cappelli drugged her and bound her paws with wire? Surely he didn't need to, but she'd wanted to get away from him for some reason. Topher hoped she was safe and longed for her to come and help him.

Chapter 13

The following days brought more lessons – and more blows from Mr Wiggins. Quiltie, a pockmarked Irish cove with red hair, gave him a lesson in his speciality – star glazing. That was sticking a knife in a shop window till a crack appeared, then taking out the pane and grabbing the goods from a display. He demonstrated on the front window of the room they all lived in while others kept watch. But Topher wasn't good at that either. He wasn't good at any sort of stealing.

'It's a pity,' said Snoop, 'because you look good as gold so no one would suspect you. But you *are* good, Toffee, that's your trouble. Too much Sunday school, that was your undoing.' Mr Squittle was getting upset, he said, because Topher wasn't earning his keep. 'Pies cost money, Toffee.'

'I empty his chamber pot.' It was a disgusting job taking it to the overflowing privy in the back yard.

'But that's not earning.'

'I read him the *Morning Chronicle*.'

'Again, *not earning*. He can't throw you out, Toffee, because you know too much. If you go on like this you'll end up in the Thames, tied to a bag of bricks. Mr Wiggins and me, we're getting it in the neck because we brought you here.'

Desperate, Topher said he could sew. His ma had taught him.

'*Phew!*' Snoop laughed. 'Your life saved by a thread, Toffee. I know what job you can do.'

From then on, Topher was made to unpick the initials on the stolen handkerchiefs and cover up the holes with neat new stitches. But reading the papers was what he liked best. That's how he kept track of the days, and that's how he learned that Ka was still free, when a WANTED poster caught his eye.

Unfortunately it caught Mr Squittle's eye too. He could read numbers. 'What's that?' He pointed to a 5 at the bottom of the page.

'It's a reward of five guineas for the return of a lost cat.'

The cat. Signor Cappelli's cat. Ka. Topher felt his heart skip a beat.

'Five guineas! That's better than billy snatching.' Mr Squittle would have toppled from his chair if Topher hadn't pushed him back in. He made him read every word and then wake up the night shift to tell them about it. It was raining but half of them shot straight out to start looking. Not Topher though, even when he said he knew the cat. Not even after Snoop came in and told Mr Squittle that Topher had a better chance of catching the cat than the others, because the cat seemed to like him. Mr Squittle said he didn't trust Topher not to run away and snitch. So it was back to chamber pot emptying and stitching and reading the papers.

That's what he was doing when, a few days later, another name he recognised soon caught his eye.

Joseph Bazalgette.

It seemed her majesty had a problem with doodahs, though the newspaper called it 'sewage' and 'excrement'. At high tide the waste flowed back up the sewers into the cellars under Buckingham Palace, meaning that her majesty's delicate nostrils were assailed by a terrible pong. The whole palace ponged, so she'd ordered the Prime Minister to do something about it.

And he had, because the toffs in the Houses of Parliament were very upset too. They'd been upset ever since the day they had been driven from the Houses by the Great Stink emanating from the Thames, creating a foul miasma.

Emanating was a new word to Topher, so was *miasma*, but he remembered the day the newspaper was talking of vividly. It was the day he'd escaped from the workhouse, the day Snoop had brought him here. He remembered all the folk running away from the river.

'So? What've you stopped reading for, boy?' Mr Squittle banged his crutch on the floor. 'What did the Prime Minister do?'

'He sent for Mr Bazalgette,' said Topher.

'Who's he then and what's he going to do?' said Snoop, who was listening too.

'He's an engineer and –' Topher scanned the paper – 'he's going to build bigger sewers to carry all the doodahs further down the river, away from the town.'

But Snoop had stopped listening. So had Mr Squittle, who had noticed Snoop looking out of the window.

Staring out of the window. 'What is it, Snoop?' Mr Squittle banged his crutch again.

'Five guineas,' said Snoop. 'Five golden guineas are sitting outside in the street. Or, to be more precise, Cappelli's cat is.'

'Then what are you standing there for?'

Snoop pulled a mutton-chop bone from his pocket. He must have had it there ever since he'd heard about the reward. 'Back in a minute, Mr Squittle.' As he reached the door he picked up a square basket. He must have had that ready too. Then he was off. They heard him thundering down the stairs.

Quiltie made as if to follow, but Squittle hissed, 'Sss . . . tay and keep hold of that dog.'

Streak, a white bull terrier with red eyes was always by Quiltie's side and it kept close now as he went over to the window to watch what was happening outside. So did the other coves from the night shift, who had all woken up.

When Topher was sure that Mr Squittle had lost interest in the newspaper he joined them.

The cat was on the bottom step. Topher could see it clearly. Quiltie had pushed open the sash to see better. Part of Topher wanted to yell, 'Run, cat!' But another part of him longed to see her again. Surely she'd run anyway if she wanted to. But she didn't seem to want to. She looked up at the window. At *him*. He felt Ka's eyes looking into his.

Then Snoop appeared outside with the basket, which he put down behind him. He'd taken off his coat which

69

dangled from his hand. 'Puss, puss, puss.' Crouching and moving slowly he spread his coat over the step below him. Then he held out the chop bone. 'Puss, puss, puss.'

Topher caught his breath as the cat put both forepaws on the step above, in fact onto Snoop's coat. It looked as if she was walking into his trap.

'Nice pussy.'

Ka sniffed the chop. She jumped onto the coat fully and Snoop slowly reached for the basket with his free hand. He lifted it up, and brought it round and then quickly down over the cat. 'Gotcha!' He held the basket in place with the top half of his body. Then, lifting the edges of his coat so it was covered, he straightened up and carried it carefully towards the door.

But had he got Ka? Topher wasn't sure.

Chapter 14

'Bring it here then.' Mr Squittle jerked his head as Snoop came in the door with the basket.

'Close the door and keep it closed,' he ordered Quiltie as Snoop put the basket at his feet – or where his feet would have been if he had any.

'Ta-ran-ta-ta!' Dramatically, with a finger and thumb, Snoop whipped his jacket off the basket. 'Here are your five guineas, Mr Squittle. More if...'

There was a second's silence as the old man peered inside. Then his crutch came down *thwack!* on Snoop's head.

For the next half-hour everyone was scurrying hither and thither, searching the room from top to bottom and corner to corner.

'It m-must be here,' stammered Snoop when he'd recovered enough to speak. He said he was sure he'd brought the cat inside, but Topher was sure that he hadn't. He'd seen a flurry of golden fur as Snoop lowered the basket over the cat – Ka escaping.

Furious, Mr Squittle sent Froggy and a couple more coves outside to search. Then he ordered Mr Wiggins to make discreet enquiries of the other rooms' inhabitants.

Wiggins went off, but his hopes weren't high. Topher could tell. The cove's huge shoulders were bowed. His stringy whiskers drooped. Word had got round about

Cappelli's missing cat, and about the reward. If anyone had the cat now they wouldn't tell Wiggins.

'So n-near,' Snoop dabbed at the blood trickling from the gash in his cheek.

'So far!' hissed Mr Squittle, raising his crutch again.

No one found the cat that day and Topher's life went back to its normal round of stitching, newspaper reading and emptying Mr Squittle's chamber pot. Then one night a stranger appeared, wrapped in a grey hooded cloak.

Topher had just come in from the privy. He was putting the chamber pot back behind Mr Squittle's chair when Snoop brought in the man.

Desperate to seek favour with Mr Squittle ever since the cat debacle, Snoop was almost bent double. 'Somebody to discuss business with you, Mr Squittle.' He obviously didn't want anyone else to hear.

'What is it then?'

The stranger mumbled something and Mr Squittle told everyone to leave the room, even Snoop.

Afterwards Topher wondered why he'd stayed put, crouched behind the chair, watching and listening. But by the time he thought of moving it was too late. He'd heard things neither of the two men would want him to hear.

'Let's see who I'm dealing with,' Mr Squittle growled, and the stranger opened his cloak, revealing a bald pate and red and black livery.

'My master, the Duke of Northumberland...'

'Sent you?' said Mr Squittle.

'I'm his major-domo,' said the old retainer. He went on to talk about his master's house and the northern-level lower sewers – and, to Topher's surprise, Joseph Bazalgette.

'Get to the point, man.'

'This sewer is going to plough straight through my master's property.'

'Northumberland House, at the end of The Strand?'

Topher saw the magnificent house in his mind's eye. He'd passed it several times. House wasn't the word. It was a mansion.

'Yes, and they... want to knock it down for the... *sssewers*.' The man spat out the word. 'And a newfangled underground railway.'

'Who's "they"?'

'The Metropolitan Board of Works, but it's the boss, Bazalgette, with his madcap scheme for a huge embankment...'

'So...' Mr Squittle was about to say something else but suddenly threw his crutch at the door roaring, 'Get away, you varmints!' He waited for the sound of feet running downstairs before he continued. 'Can't see why the duke's worried. He'll get compensation enough. Hundreds of pounds, if the papers are right, more than enough to build another house.'

'With respect, you're wrong, Mr Squittle. The duke won't rebuild. There won't be another house and that's why we need to do business.'

Both men lowered their voices then, but Topher

picked up the gist. The duke would not build another house because he needed the money to pay his gambling debts. All the servants, including this man, lived in Northumberland House too, so they would lose their jobs and their homes.

'If this sewer scheme goes ahead, my colleagues and I will all end up in the workhouse.'

'So what am I supposed to do about it, Mr Markely?' At some point Mr Squittle must have learned the cove's name.

'Get...'

'Who? What? Speak up, man.'

Topher hadn't heard the name either but did when Mr Markely said it again.

'Get *Bazalgette*, the cove in charge of operations, the driving force. He chose this scheme. He's pushing it through. Stop him, stop this. Then the board will choose another project that don't involve destroying my master's house.'

'And you want me to arrange this cove's... disposal?'

Mr Markely must have nodded because Mr Squittle said, 'That would be very expensive, Mr Markely. How would you pay?'

'With this?'

Topher heard the chink of metal against metal and, leaning to the side slightly, caught sight of two silver spoons.

'Solid silver, Mr Squittle, not plate and there's more where they came from.'

'There would need to be, Mr Markely, and I'd need to see more before I start making arrangements.' Mr Squittle pulled his spyglass out of his pocket and examined one of the spoons before handing it back.

Shortly afterwards, the Duke of Northumberland's major-domo pulled up his hood, wrapped his cloak around him and left the room. And Topher, crouched behind Mr Squittle's chair, wondered when he could safely emerge, or if he was safe where he was. He was scared that the man could hear his heart beating. His head was full of questions. Had a deal been struck? He knew the old soldier was a fence. Topher had seen him use that spyglass many times to examine the hallmarks on stolen silver. But was he into murder too? Had he just agreed to arrange the 'disposal' of Joseph Bazalgette?

Chapter 15

It was a while before the other coves returned. Only then did Topher stand up as casually as he could, hoping no one had noticed he hadn't been outside with them.

Snoop said, 'Where did you get to then, Toffee? Thought you'd scarpered, I did. Thought better of it, did yer? Wise cove.'

Mr Squittle seemed to be asleep in his chair – though it was hard to tell – but he didn't seem to know his conversation with Mr Markely had been overheard. Murder, that's what they'd talked about, cold-blooded murder. Now Topher remembered what Snoop had said about tying him to a bag of bricks and throwing him in the Thames. Clearly he hadn't been joking. He fingered Mr Bazalgette's card, still in his pocket. He'd be in trouble if the others found this. He remembered how kind the gentleman had been. He thought about his little daughter. She'd lose her dad if Mr Markely got his way. So he must warn him. But how? The only time he got outside was when he went to the privy in the back yard, but the gate there was locked and the walls too high to climb over.

There was just one glimmer of hope. Mr Squittle hadn't said he definitely would do the terrible deed. He'd said only if Mr Markely brought him more silver. So, if the major-domo didn't bring him any the deal was off.

Topher formed a plan. If Mr Markely did come back, and if Mr Squittle told everyone to leave the room as he had today, Topher would make sure he left with them. Then he'd try and give the others the slip and leave the house. Then he'd make his way to the police station in Bow Street, or even their headquarters in Scotland Yard, or Mr Bazalgette's offices in George Street, though he wasn't sure where that was. Trouble was, he'd never ever managed to leave the house before, and it wasn't for lack of trying. But there was always someone around to stop him.

For several days life went on as usual and Topher's hopes for Mr Bazalgette rose. Mr Markely didn't return, and now, when he read the *Morning Chronicle* or *Illustrated London News* to Mr Squittle, Topher kept coming across the name Joseph Bazalgette. The man was an inspiration to rich and poor alike. He was a modern-day hero who was going to defeat the monster cholera, not with sword and shield, but with his 'intercepting system of drainage'. The dry words now sounded fascinating to Topher. Mr Bazalgette was going to build *eighty-three miles* of huge new brick sewers to intercept the sewage outflow and *one thousand miles* of smaller sewers to carry away the waste. Instead of flowing along the streets of London for everyone to see and smell and catch diseases from, all the doodahs would stay under the ground till they'd nearly reached the sea. Well, Bazalgette was going to get the sewers built, not actually build them himself, but he'd designed the system and was going to make sure it was built exactly according to his plan. It would cost three million pounds, but would save thousands of lives and everyone, well almost everyone, was in favour. There would never be another Great Stink. London would be a cleaner, healthier place for everyone. There might even be fish swimming in the River Thames one day.

One morning another familiar name in the newspaper caught Topher's eye, *Broad Street* – that was where he used to live. Now he read that it was the scene of a famous discovery! A man called Dr John Snow, a great supporter of Mr Bazalgette, had proved four years ago that drinking water that contained sewage caused cholera. The doctor had traced the disease back to one pump on Broad Street infected by an overflowing privy. Families who used that pump got cholera. Families who used a different pump didn't.

'Wotcha stopped reading for, Toffee?' Snoop poked him. 'Mr Squittle's waiting.'

Topher had stopped because he was remembering and the words had blurred with tears. His tears came because *his family* had used that infected pump on Broad Street. They must have. Why he himself hadn't died he'd never know because the rest of his family had. He'd come home one day to find his little sister Bessie crying that she had a terrible tummy ache. Then she'd started being sick, then her skin turned blue, and most horrible of all, she'd started twitching. He'd never forget the spasms of twitching. One minute her arms and legs were still, next they were jumping all over the place and her teeth were chattering. Even after she'd died she'd gone on twitching for a bit. Then his ma got the same thing, and his da and his three little brothers, and within a fortnight they were all in the churchyard.

Snoop poked him. 'Start reading again, Toffee, if yer don't want a sore head.' He nodded in the direction of Mr Squittle, who was clutching his crutch ominously.

'*Her majesty has also given her blessing to Mr Bazalgette's project*,' read Topher quickly, '*and Mr Benjamin Disraeli, the Chancellor of the Exchequer, has made funds available. Work will start at the very first opportunity.*'

Later, while he was sewing by the window, Topher couldn't stop thinking about Mr Bazalgette. His new sewers would stop a lot of misery. They would stop a lot of people dying. But not if he were murdered.

So Topher's heart sank when Snoop came in that very night with a heavy box wrapped in brown paper. 'A present from a certain gentleman,' he said mysteriously, putting it in front of Mr Squittle.

He told Snoop to undo it.

So off came the string and brown paper and out came a fine silver plate. Mr Squittle examined the hallmark using his spyglass. Then he grunted and Snoop handed him a silver jug.

'Good stuff, Mr Squittle? Yes? Then I have a message for you.' Snoop leaned over and whispered in Mr Squittle's ear.

Not long afterwards Mr Squittle asked Snoop for a

street map and was soon poring over it, while Topher stood beside him holding a candle. Neither of the men mentioned it but he knew that the plot to murder Mr Bazalgette was now under way. That was obvious. Snoop was part of it. So was Wiggins and Mr Squittle's old comrade from the Crimea, Army McAvoy.

They got down to detail the next morning, after the day-shift team had gone out, but first Mr Wiggins sent Topher to sit by the window.

'You get on with your stitching, Toffee.'

Then the four thieves went into a huddle by the fire. From the corner of his eye, Topher saw Wiggins take out his cosh, and Snoop his knife. He strained to hear, but caught only murmurs and mutters. Then Wiggins tapped the cosh against the palm of his hand as if testing its weight and looked in Topher's direction. Suddenly there was quite a lot of looking in his direction. *Too much.* He could feel them all staring even when he kept his head down, which he did all the time now – and he started to feel uneasy. Did they suspect that he knew? He told himself they were just checking he wasn't listening, but then he heard the floorboards creak and knew someone was walking towards him.

'It's your lucky day, Toffee,' said Snoop, grinning like a gargoyle. Topher knew lucky wasn't the word.

Chapter 16

Mr Wiggins joined Snoop. 'We've got a treat for you, Toffee. Mr Squittle is going to trust you to do an errand for him. Show him the picture, Snoop.'

Snoop held out a picture of a man with dark wavy hair and distinctive triangle-shaped side-whiskers. It was, of course, Joseph Bazalgette. 'All you've got to do is take a message to this fine gentleman. You're to tell him that his friend, Mr Isambard Kingdom Brunel is er... desirous of meeting him for luncheon at Verrey's in Regent Street. Got that?'

'Both coves are Frenchies,' added Snoop. 'It's a Frenchy eating place. They like French nosh, these posh coves do.'

Mr Bazalgette is as English as you are. I've heard him talking. But Topher didn't say that. He didn't say anything. Best let them think he was stupid.

Wiggins continued, 'Tell the gentleman that Mr Brunel says it's very important and you'll take him to save time. Say you know a short cut.' He spread the map of London in front of him and pointed to an alley between two streets. 'There's the short cut. Remember that.'

Because you'll be waiting with your cosh. And Snoop with his knife most like.

'Er... I think it would be better if Snoop went. I'm not sure I could find it.'

81

Snoop shook his head slowly. 'Toffee, I don't think you understand. Mr Squittle is doing you a favour. Turn this down and you might never get out of here again – alive.'

Mr Wiggins nodded. 'Now listen, we're going to kit you out in smart togs, and if you do this right and prove yourself trustworthy Mr Squittle might let you do other jobs.'

Topher's brain was working overtime. Could this be his only chance to warn Mr Bazalgette? 'When do you want me to do this?' He ought to find out as much as he could about their plan.

'We'll tell you when.' Wiggins ruffled Topher's hair. 'Good job your golden locks have grown a bit, so you don't look as if you're from the workhouse. Now get on with your stitching.'

The men walked back to Mr Squittle, who called him over a few minutes later too, handing him the *Morning Chronicle*. 'This intercepting system of drainage, I'd like to know more about that.'

Of course, Topher knew that Squittle really wanted to know about Joseph Bazalgette, and most particularly *where* he was working. Fortunately – or unfortunately – the paper made clear that the site was quite close. The engineer was supervising the surveying of the north bank of the Thames, all the way from Westminster Bridge to Blackfriars Bridge. Sometimes he went on foot. Sometimes, because part of the huge embankment was going to be built on the riverbed, he boarded a barge. It was an amazing construction.

Topher pretended not to take any notice when Mr Squittle sent Snoop and Froggy out after he'd finished reading. But it was obvious that he'd sent them out to find the famous man and follow him.

Then Wiggins came over with the map and a pencil. 'This is the route you must take to the restaurant. Now, remember what you have to say to the gentleman?'

'Er... Mr Brunel, I've got a message from a friend...'

'*NO!*' Mr Wiggins went over the plan again. He gave Topher an idea.

'Sorry, Mr Wiggins. Nerves got the better of me. Think perhaps we should have a trial run? To make sure I do it right?'

Unfortunately Mr Wiggins rightly suspected Topher's motive. 'And give you a chance to do a runner?' he scoffed. 'Not that you'd get very far.' He patted the cosh in his pocket.

Topher had another idea later while folding up the map. On the back it said it had been produced 'so that passengers in hansom cabs could check that they were being taken by the shortest route'. Well, if he could get Mr Bazalgette inside a hansom cab the man would be safe from Wiggins's cosh and Snoop's knife. He started to rehearse what he'd say to the man as soon as he got close enough. '*Your life is in danger, sir. I have come to warn you. Please, show no sign of distress, but walk with me and summon a hansom cab as soon as you can.*' Would he have time to do that? Would *he* be able to get in the cab with Mr Bazalgette? If he didn't he'd most likely feel the cosh on his own head.

He was still going over these words in his head the next evening when Wiggins gave him a bundle of clothes.

'Try these on, Toffee.'

There were breeches, boots, a shirt and a tweed jacket, most likely stolen from a young toff who'd left them in a pile while he swam in the Serpentine in Hyde Park.

And they fitted. Topher felt good in them and even better when Mr Wiggins said he'd changed his mind about a trial run.

'Mr Squittle thinks it's a good idea. Have a dress rehearsal, that's what he thinks. So tomorrow you're going to go out with Snoop so he can show you the way. And someone who looks a bit like the cove you've got to talk to will be standing there, so you can say what you've got to say, and do what you've got to do without feeling nervy like.'

Great. Topher just hoped he'd be able to give Snoop the slip so he could make his way to the police station.

But Snoop was suspicious from the moment they stepped out of the door. 'Don't forget Slim, Toffee.' Snoop's hand was on his knife, and his eyes were riveted on Topher.

Perhaps that's why the thief didn't see the cat. Or maybe it was just the smoky air.

But Topher saw her. Ka. It was definitely her, peeping out from behind the gatepost of the house opposite. He recognised the mark on her forehead, though she was only there for a second.

Snoop opened the gate onto the street. 'Good to be out, eh, Toffee? Go on, walk in front of me and look as if you're enjoying yourself.' He started kicking the leaves piled in the gutter.

Topher saw that while he'd been locked inside the Rookery, summer had turned to chilly autumn.

The cat appeared again briefly when they reached Charing Cross. He and Snoop were standing in front of the horse statue when he heard a little mew. Turning, he saw Ka behind the horse's hind leg – for a second. It was as if she made sure he saw her and that Snoop didn't. That's what he couldn't help thinking, and it made him feel a bit hopeful. The cat was *on his side*. The cat was helping him somehow, he just knew it.

Luckily Snoop's attention was elsewhere. He was waiting for someone, that was obvious, and he was jumpy. Topher started to feel suspicious. Was this really a dress rehearsal?

Then Froggy stepped out from behind one of the waiting stagecoaches, his breath adding to the fog. 'He's on Waterman's Pier,' he hissed.

'Then that's where we're heading. Come on, Toffee. You tell Ginger, Froggy.'

This wasn't a dress rehearsal. The urgency in their voices made that clear.

Glad they thought him so stupid that they weren't even trying to keep their plan secret any more, Topher followed Snoop onto The Strand. Heading east, they soon passed Northumberland Place where the duke had his big house.

Further down Snoop turned into a road on the right. 'George Street. Here we are. Remember your lines, Toffee?'

Topher was wondering if they were near Mr Bazalgette's office, when he saw the cat again. Briefly. She dived behind a wall topped by railings just as he caught a whiff of the river. The stench wasn't as bad as it had been that day in the middle of summer, but it was bad enough to make him hold his nose.

Snoop seemed not to notice the cat or the stench. He was going faster now, towards the pier at the end of the street.

As they got nearer Topher could make out men with tripods and plumb lines and measuring rods. A gentleman in a top hat was leaning over the railing. In the river below, a man in a rowing boat shouted, 'That enough for you, Mr Bazalgette?'

Snoop started, but Topher pretended he hadn't heard. He was sure now, though. He wasn't meeting 'someone who looked like the cove'. It *was* the cove, Joseph Bazalgette, and if he didn't keep his wits about him he was going to lead him to his death.

A man, *the* man – the one in the top hat – called, 'Thank you, James, that will do for now!'

Topher saw that he must move quickly and get onto the pier to deliver his lines, *his* lines, the ones he'd made up, so Snoop couldn't hear what he said.

'Yes, Snoop, I know my lines,' he said, answering the cove's earlier question. He stepped forward.

But Snoop grabbed his arm. 'Not so fast, Toffee.

When the cove walks off the pier, that's when you say your piece.' He kept tight hold.

Then, looking round, Topher noticed Ginger and Froggy and another of Squittle's gang, not far off, surrounding him. When Mr Bazalgette walked off the pier he'd be surrounded too.

'Now, Toffee,' Snoop murmured in his ear. 'Go and do your party piece. Give the gentleman the message if you don't want to feel Slim between your ribs.'

Chapter 17

'Go on.' Snoop gave him a shove.

Topher stepped forward and saw Mr Bazalgette pull a gold watch from the pocket of his yellow waistcoat. Then the clatter of hooves made the engineer, and everyone else, turn to look down George Street, where a hansom cab pulled by a chestnut mare was rolling towards them. A whiff of horse sweat filled Topher's nose as the mare rushed past and drew up in front of the great man.

'Three minutes late,' he heard Mr Bazalgette say to the driver. '17 Hamilton Terrace, St John's Wood, as fast as you can. I'm hungry and my luncheon awaits.'

Topher tried to stop himself smiling as the cab rolled away before he'd been able to say anything. It was as if what he'd planned was happening without his help. Mr Bazalgette was safe.

But *he* wasn't.

'Take that smile off your face, glock.' Snoop wrenched Topher's head back and laid the knife across his throat. 'What do you think Mr Squittle will say about this, Toffee? *When* are you going to learn to do what you're told?'

''S'not my fault.' Topher was expecting the blade to slice through his windpipe when, from the corner of his eye, he caught a glimpse of something that could change everything.

Ka! The cat was sitting on a post at the entrance to the pier. Watching. Waiting. Staring their way. Not hiding. She seemed to want them all to see her.

'L-look, Snoop, C-Cappelli's cat.'

'And pigs flying, eh, Toffee?' Snoop didn't look and tightened his grip.

'No really, Snoop.' Topher managed to point with his free hand.

Snoop must have looked and seen because a low whistle escaped from his lips. 'Nice one, Toffee.'

'F-five guineas,' said Topher, feeling like a traitor. 'That would m-make Mr Squittle feel better.'

Snoop obviously agreed. Lowering the knife, he looked round to where Froggy, Ginger and the third cove were standing, all focussed on Topher, all strategically placed to stop him escaping. But could they stop a cat? Clearly they didn't know they had to. They hadn't seen Ka yet and were confused by Snoop's pointing finger. 'Get the cat!' he yelled, and at last they caught on.

Slowly they started to move in on Ka till they were close enough to hear Snoop giving directions.

'Softly softly, boys. Main thing is she mustn't come this way. If we can drive her back onto the pier we've got her, unless she can swim.'

The three started to move forward.

Topher could hardly believe that the cat was just sitting there, waiting. Nor could he believe that Snoop seemed to have forgotten all about him. The cat had been playing *Now you see me, Now you don't* all day but now she just sat and her amber eyes seemed to look straight into his. *Go on, escape. Run.* The words suddenly came into his head. Was that what she was telling him? Scarper while he had the chance?

But what if Snoop heard and turned round? He was only yards away. If he heard Topher's boots hitting the cobbles, he might send the knife flying into his back.

Deciding to move softly softly himself, Topher took one step backwards, keeping watch on the cat and the three coves creeping up on her.

'What we going to put it in?' he heard Froggy say.

Snoop barked, 'Take off your coat.' He still had Slim in his hand and Topher immediately guessed his plan. Throw the coat over the cat. Then pin it down with the help of the knife. But what if he missed and knifed the cat? The thought made Topher flinch.

Ka still sat, washing herself now, as if she hadn't a care in the world.

But Topher felt sure she was watching.

He took another step backwards. It was like the game Grandma's footsteps in reverse. A few more steps and he'd reach the buildings in George Street and if he took a few steps sideways maybe he could find a hiding place. Or should he change direction and head for the riverbank?

Now, the three would-be cat catchers were very close to their prey. He could see Froggy's coat trailing from his right hand. He watched the lad lift the coat so he was holding it in front of him with both hands. Then suddenly Froggy was flying towards the cat, landing flat on the wooden floor of the pier. 'Gotcha!'

90

But he hadn't. Ka, a flurry of golden fur, was twisting away from them in the air.

'Idiot! That way!' Snoop pointed as the cat landed and ran. But then he remembered Topher, and Topher, now running beside the river, heard him shout. 'Toffee, stop! Or Mr Squittle will cut off your ears!'

But of course Topher didn't stop. Wasn't Scotland Yard wharf only a few hundred yards west? If he kept running he'd come to it and then it shouldn't take him long to find the police headquarters.

But that wasn't as easy as it had first seemed. The path was getting muddier and soon disappeared completely. Must be high tide. The Thames was sloshing over the bank. He splashed his way through. He could see a brick building ahead blocking his way. Some sort of warehouse, with a pier alongside it and folks below were unloading a wherry and attaching the cargo to a crane. Worse, there seemed to be buildings for as far as he could see, littering the riverbank with fences and rough ground between them. No path. Topher stopped to think, but not for long.

'Toffee, don't be a glock!' He turned to see Snoop coming after him, hat in hand.

What now? He couldn't go forward or backwards or left into the river. So there was only one option. Turning sharp right he headed inland, not very fast because the ground was rough, but as fast as he could, because Snoop had turned too and was trying to cut off his escape route. There were buildings ahead, houses possibly, running parallel with The Strand.

'Toffee, stop!' Snoop was gaining ground, but the buildings were now in reach. There was an alley straight ahead, between two blocks of houses. Diving into it, he ran till he came to a opening, turned, and turned again into another alley, trying to throw Snoop off his scent. He felt like a rabbit in a warren, being pursued by a fox.

''Scuse me, fellahs.' Topher wove his way round two coves who were blocking his path, one with a ferret looped over his arm.

As he ran past grimy back yards, he caught glimpses of women hanging out their washing and men chopping wood. Oh, no! Now his way was blocked by a cove dragging a pig on a rope. Best go back the way he'd come. But there was another cove with a barrow behind him. He was caught in the middle. Couldn't go forward. Couldn't go back.

And there was Snoop coming into the alley.

''Scuse me.' Topher dived through the nearest gate into a yard, where a wrinkled old crone stood in her doorway looking at a pile of logs and a sawhorse. Had Snoop seen him? That was the question. Slamming the gate shut and leaning against it, he heard his pursuer's voice.

'Seen a young cove, smartly dressed, have you? Running this way?'

'What's it worth, mate?' said one of the coves.

Gasping for breath, Topher waited for Snoop's reply.

'The blighter stole my old lady's purse.'

'Purse?' the old crone hissed in his ear.

'That a way then,' said one of the coves in the alley.

Was he pointing into the yard? The old woman obviously thought he might be. With surprising quickness she bolted the gate and grasped Topher's shoulders.

'Purse. Where is it then?'

'I haven't got one,' said Topher. 'I didn't steal anything.'

He could feel her bony fingers digging into him. 'Empty your pockets.'

He turned them inside out, revealing all of nothing, and she spat on the ground. Then she yelled, 'Podger, come and turn this whippersnapper upside-down!'

As a brawny fellow appeared in the doorway of the house, Topher took a look at the gate. Could he get out before the man reached him?

Mwow!

Ka was on the top of the gate.

Topher threw himself at it, rammed back the bolt and opened it, slammed it shut then stepped out into the alley.

The coves had gone. So had the pig. So had Snoop. But Ka was waiting.

'*R . . . rrrrrrun!*'

She raced to the left and Topher followed her as if his life depended on it.

Because it did.

Podger was now coming out of the gate brandishing an axe.

Chapter 18

Ka's paws hardly touched the ground.

He saw her disappear round a corner – oh, no! – but when he turned it she was waiting, checking that he was following, before she bounded off again. Where was she going? Topher soon lost track. There were so many houses. The alleys between the blocks were a maze. High brick walls on either side shut out the light, but at least there weren't too many folk about. When he heard church clocks striking one, he thought most people must be inside scratching around for something to eat.

Another good thing, Ka seemed to know where she was going. She really was clever. She *thought*. He could tell from the way she looked at him. And the cat definitely knew these alleys. But so – unfortunately – did Podger.

'I'll catch yer, yer varmint!' The brawny fellow wasn't far behind.

From time to time Topher could hear him yelling, hear his nailed boots hitting the cobbles, but luckily the fellow wasn't fleet of foot. Ka was and as Topher doubled his efforts to keep up with her, the sounds of Podger grew fainter and fainter.

Faster. Faster. Topher urged himself on and there, at last, was a main road ahead, blocked with carts and carriages. The Strand, it must be, and there was Ka standing on the edge of the road, waiting.

She looked up at him. '*Rrr...eady?*'

'Wait a minute.' He needed time to catch his breath. But she didn't think they had time.

'*Rrrr...eady?*' This time the cat didn't wait for an answer but made a dash. And Topher forced himself to follow, weaving in and out of wheels higher than himself and the legs of horses with huge fetlocked hooves.

'Stop!' He heard Podger yell as he reached the middle of the road. So Ka had been right. Of course she had. He staggered on till he reached the other side, only then glancing back to see the fat fellow stranded. There was no way someone his size could squeeze between the coaches.

Mwow! Ka was at his feet. Her message was clear: *Don't linger. Come on.*

She headed west now, towards Charing Cross, and didn't stop when they got there. Turning right, Ka led the way between the stationary coaches, lifting her paws high to keep them above the horse dung. Good. She was heading north now. If she'd gone left towards Cockspur he'd have been even more worried. He didn't want to run into to anybody from the Rookery. By now, Snoop would most like have got word to the others that he had escaped, and that their plan to murder Mr Bazalgette had failed. So he kept a look out for members of the so-called family.

Mwow! Come on! Ka was already in Trafalgar Square.

It was nearly empty, just a few bystanders were looking up at the statue of Lord Nelson.

Ka checked that Topher was still following, and then raced across the square, corner to corner, scattering pigeons in her wake.

He followed but not at a run because he couldn't. He'd been cooped up so long that he wasn't used to running. Ka was waiting on the corner of the Mall.

'Going to see the queen, are you?' Topher knew Buckingham Palace wasn't far away.

Two hansom cabs rolled past, one pulled by a chestnut mare. Was Mr Bazalgette in it?

Mwow! Come on!

Where *was* Ka going?

She turned into the Haymarket, then down a side road and then another. Soon they were in another maze of small streets, but – he was almost certain – they were still heading north. Could she be going where he hoped she was? To warn Mr Bazalgette of the plot to kill him? Had she heard the gentleman give his address to the hansom cab driver? 17 Hamilton Terrace, St John's Wood. Did she know where that was? If only they could take a cab. Topher was exhausted.

The only good thing was that Podger seemed to have given up the chase, but Ka hadn't slowed down. She disappeared into a cut between two red-brick houses. He reached the cut and staggered after her. It was like a tunnel. Dark. He couldn't see Ka, but he suddenly had to stop, gasping for breath, doubled up with a stitch jabbing his side.

But then she was back, rubbing her fur against his face, purring in his ear. *Rrrrr. Rrrrr…*

'Thanks, I've got to rest, Ka.'

But he had misunderstood. Now she tugged at his sleeve with her teeth. She didn't mean rest. '*Rrrrr... un. Rrrrr...un.*'

He managed to stand up.

'*Rrrrr. Rrrrr.*' She sounded urgent.

'Warn Mr Bazalgette? Yes, I know.'

She made a little run forwards. Then stopped to stare back at him. Her message was clear. *Come on.*

'Sorry, Ka.' He tried to stand up but needed more time to recover. If they *were* going to warn Mr Bazalgette there was a long way to go. St John's Wood was another two miles away, at least.

'*Rrrrrrrrrrr.*' The cat was growling and tugging his trouser bottoms. '*Run!*'

Topher struggled to his feet, using the wall for support, but it was too late.

'Toffee.' Snoop's voice was unmistakable and so was his long thin shape at the far end of the cut. 'With the famous pussy cat.'

Topher turned to run back but saw that someone else was blocking the exit.

Podger.

Chapter 19

Podger turned Topher upside-down.

'You've got that purse somewhere.'

Head inches from the ground, Topher saw boots coming towards him, and a dangling net. Snoop, creeping up on Ka. But where was she?

Then Podger started shaking him from side to side like a dog with a rat in its mouth. When the purse didn't fall to the ground he wrenched off Topher's jacket. 'I'll strip you naked if I have to.'

Topher pedalled his legs as hard as he could, trying to land a kick. He pummelled the fellow with his free hand, but to such a solid cove, his blows were like flies landing on a dung heap. Next Podger started yanking at his breeches, but suddenly the big man's grip loosened and he uttered a howl of pain.

Looking up, Topher now saw a faceless Podger. Ka was covering it, clinging to it with her claws. Then she was sliding slowly downwards, etching the thug's face with long bloody scratches. Then – *thunk* – Topher's head hit the ground as Podger dropped him. Sick filled his mouth then spilled out of it as he howled with pain.

And everything went black.

When he opened his eyes everything was still black and Topher wondered if he'd died and gone to hell. Then he saw stars above him. Were there stars in hell? Something touched his face and he started. A rat? No.

'Ka!' Two green eyes shone out of the darkness. 'Clever Ka.' He remembered his last sight of her. 'You gave him a good scratching.'

She rubbed her face against his, purring ecstatically. *Rrrrr. Rrrrr.* She seemed thrilled to see him awake.

'Did you think I was dead? So did I.'

So did his pursuers most like or they wouldn't have left him. He felt the top of his head and found a bump the size of a potato throbbing beneath his fingers. Now he realised his head was aching but he *was* alive.

'Thank you, Ka.' She had saved him.

But where was Podger? Where was Snoop? Had they really gone? He struggled into a sitting position and stared into the darkness. He strained his ears for the sound of their voices, but all he could hear was the cat's urgent purring.

'*Hu . . . rrrrr . . . y. Hu . . . rrrrrr . . . y.*' She tugged at his shirt. '*Wa . . . rrrrr . . . n. Wa . . . rrrrr . . . n.*'

Warn? Who? '*Who?*' But even as he asked, the gentleman's face came into Topher's mind. Eyebrows like dark furry caterpillars over kindly eyes. Triangular whiskers. Ka was thinking about Mr Bazalgette. The man was still in danger. They ought to be heading for his house. That's where Snoop and Wiggins and co would be going. If they hadn't already got there.

Shivering in the cold autumn night, Topher felt around the cobbles for his jacket but couldn't find it. Most likely Podger or Snoop had taken it. He struggled to his feet and when the walls stopped spinning, realised his feet were bare. The thieving coves had taken his boots too.

'Come on then, Ka. 17 Hamilton Terrace. That's where we're heading. You'll have to lead the way though.'

He still felt unsteady on his feet. The thump on his head hadn't done him any good at all.

Ka set off again, and though the moon came out from behind a cloud, he found it hard to see her when she went ahead. But she seemed to know that and kept closer than she had before. What time was it? He had no idea till he heard a clock striking and stopped to count. Seven o'clock.

'*Hu...rrrrr...y. Hu...rrrrr...y.*'

But he couldn't go very fast.

Eventually cobbled streets and houses gave way to rougher open ground. The bushes and trees slowed him down even more. Forcing himself to keep going, he followed the cat, though his body was yearning for sleep.

Save Mr Bazalgette. He urged himself on. *Save Mr Bazalgette.*

But what if Snoop and co had got to his house first? They'd had hours. Topher tried to put himself in their shoes. They would be scared to go back to Mr Squittle saying his plan had failed. He would be furious. So they would try again to murder the famous engineer.

How? That was the question. He thought of Wiggins's cosh and Snoop's knife.

Then, *Mwow!* Ka came to a halt at a junction.

There was a main road in front of them, quite busy for this time of night. As they waited for a carriage to pass, Topher tried to get his bearings. They must be heading north again. The road going from left to right could be Oxford Street, but the one crossing it was narrower than Regent Street. So this wasn't Oxford Circus but it could be the junction further west where Baker Street met Oxford Street. If it was they were even closer than he hoped, only a mile from St John's Wood.

Only a mile! At the best of times that would take him ten minutes, but these were the worst of times. It was dark and he was tired and cold and barefoot, and he had no idea where Snoop and Wiggins and the rest of Squittle's mob were. If they were intent on killing Mr Bazalgette they could have surrounded his house already. They could be hiding in his garden or in the street outside, waiting for him to step out of his front door. Or they might be planning to break in and murder him in his bed.

'Do you know where his house is, Ka?' he whispered into the darkness, not mentioning the man's name.

'*Of cou ... rrrrrr ... se.*'

How did she know? How clever she was. He remembered the billboard outside the theatre. 'Can you talk Italian and Chinese as well?'

But she was intent on hurrying, till a strange trumpeting howl stopped them both in their tracks. Topher guessed that Regent's Park was up ahead, which meant the Zoological Gardens were too. The noise must be one of the strange beasts from a foreign land.

101

Ka set off again.

The road was lined with trees and there were no houses. Topher did feel safer here than in the back streets, but not by much. Trees made good hiding places and so did the bridges they had to cross. So did the darkness. When the moon came out from behind a cloud he could see water glimmering, sometimes to the right of the road, sometimes the left. He thought the road followed the path of the River Tyburn winding its way down to the Thames. It was uphill all the way, slowing him down even more.

'*Hu...rrrrrr...y. Hu...rrrrr...y.*' Ka tugged at his breeches.

'I – can't – Ka.' Panting now, Topher was tired and his head hurt and he couldn't remember when he'd last had anything to eat.

'*Hu...rrrrrr...y. Hu...rrrrr...y. Dangerrrrr...*'

How much did Ka know? he wondered. Had she heard Snoop and Wiggins talking about their plans while they thought he was dead?

'What sort of danger?'

'*Mur...rrrr...der.*'

It was only what Topher already knew, but the word made him shudder. And that was before he saw three shapes ahead, three human shapes that he recognised. One was wide and bulky, one long and thin and the third was short with sticking-out elbows and a head too small for his body.

Less than a hundred yards away were Wiggins, Snoop and Froggy.

Chapter 20

Topher froze.

So did Ka, but she recovered more quickly. Streaking to the right, she disappeared. Where had she gone? He could see the three heads very clearly, too clearly. If they turned round...

Then he saw Ka's green eyes. Using them as a guide he found her behind a bush. Crouching beside the cat, he watched the silhouettes of the three conspirators get smaller and smaller until they merged with the darkness. Then he listened to the thud and shuffle of their boots till they faded completely and all he could hear was the wind sighing.

'They'll get there first,' he whispered when he was sure they'd gone. 'If only we could get ahead of them.'

Ka looked at him thoughtfully, then ran off again, but back the way they had come.

'Not that way. We need to get *ahead* of them.'

But she kept going till they came to a bridge they had crossed earlier.

He caught her up. There was water below them.

'*Trrr...ust me.*' She started to make her way down the muddy bank.

Slipping and sliding Topher followed, scared he was going to fall in. The water smelled bad, not as bad as the Thames on a hot day, but there was a definite whiff of sewage. He reached the bottom of the bank where she was waiting.

'*Ca . . . rrrrr . . . y.*' She sprang into his arms.

'Why?'

'*Enter . . . rrr.*'

'What?' He didn't understand.

'*Sewer . . . rrr. Enter . . . rrr sewer . . . rrr.*' She spoke clearly. There was no mistaking what she was saying now.

'Where?' But he saw it before the word was even out of his mouth. A sewer pipe was emptying into the Tyburn. That's where the pong came from. Now he could see doodahs floating on the surface, some of them glimmering with an eery golden glow.

'But . . .'

'*Hur . . . rrr . . . y.*' Ka nosed open his shirt and settled herself inside. '*Hur . . . rrr . . . y.*' She peeped out.

He couldn't believe what she wanted him to do.

'*Hur . . . rrry.*'

So he lowered himself into the filthy water and waded towards the sewer entrance. He peered inside the round hole. This was an old sewage pipe. It wasn't even big enough for him to stand upright, he'd have to bend double. He couldn't see inside either, not beyond the first row of bricks lining the entrance. Blackness. That's all there was, a stinking blackness.

'I'm not a tosher,' he said. He knew about the tosher boys who scavenged the sewers looking for valuables. They found stuff sometimes, but searching among all the doodahs – what sort of job was that?

'*Hur...rrr...y.*' Ka pawed at his stomach, not scratching exactly, but letting him know she could.

'I can't.' Toshers carried lamps. 'And what about Mr Bazalgette?' He pictured Wiggins, Snoop and Froggy hurrying along the highway to the famous man's house. They might even have already reached it.

'*Sho...rrr...t cut. Sho...rrr...t cut.*'

'Short cut?'

'*Undergr...rrr...ound.*'

'Through the sewers?'

'*Hu...rry.*' She gave him a nip, not hard, but enough to make him take notice, and he did. He crouched inside the sewer – because now he heard footsteps.

Ka had probably heard them earlier.

Down here in the sewer they sounded even louder. They rang in his ears. They were coming from the south, from central London. They most like belonged to more of the Rookery gang. Wiggins would have sent runners out by now. He did that when he wanted more of them to distract some poor soul while he was robbed.

But now it was for murder.

Desperate for fresh air, Topher stepped out of the sewer and peered up the bank to the road. There was a light moving, bobbing about. A lantern!

'We could do with that, Ka.' He stepped back inside.

'*Stay he...rrr...e.*' He felt her hind paws thrust against his stomach as she sprang out of his arms.

He could only guess what happened next. Hearing the murmur of voices and footsteps getting closer he

105

decided to hide under the bridge. He'd suffocate from the smell if he stayed in the sewer. If he stood under the middle of it, the villains couldn't see him even if they did lean over the sides to look. But he'd have to be quick. They were getting nearer. Then he heard the whine of a dog. Then another voice telling it to pipe down. Sounded like Quiltie and his bull terrier, Streak. Who was the other one – or two? The bridge creaked as someone stepped onto it. Then someone else. And now the lamplight showed up the gaps between the planks. He was much too near to whoever was holding it. Now there were feet just above his head, and they stopped. If the coves looked down they might see him.

'Blooming hell!' That was Quiltie. 'Shut it, Streak. It's Cappelli's cat.'

Someone whistled. 'Five golden guineas.'

'Waiting for us.'

'We can't stop to catch a cat.' That was another angry voice – Army McAvoy's – so there were *three* coves up there.

'It's not a cat. It's *the* cat,' Quiltie said again. 'And *I'm* not going without it.'

Topher couldn't believe that Ka was up there, so close to a dog. He could hear it half choking as it strained at the leash. Streak was a fighting dog and could kill her with a bite.

'Come on,' said Army. 'We've got other work to do.'

'No, not till we've got the cat.' Quiltie again. 'You know Mr Squittle wants it. Look, it's washing itself now.

106

Don't even think it's seen us. If we all creep up on it, softly softly, then make a grab, one of us is sure to get it.'

'What you going to put it in?'

'I've got a bag in my pocket. Here.'

'You'd better tie up the dog.'

'And you put the lantern down. We need three pairs of hands.'

Someone, Army he thought, placed the light inches from Topher, but impossible to get hold of unless, unless...he could make one of those gaps in the bridge bigger. If some of the wood was rotten...

'Ready?' said Quiltie.

Hearing them move towards Ka, Topher started to pick and push at the wood. Some of it *was* rotten. He had to get the lantern. Had to. Ka was doing a good job distracting the men – had this been her plan all along? – but he couldn't expect her to get the lamp herself. She was clever but she was a cat – with paws not hands. He made a gap big enough to see through. Saw her washing herself, but he was sure she was keeping an eye on her would-be catchers. He saw them converging on her. Saw their shadows cover her. Surely she'd make a run for it soon? Question was, would the coves set off in pursuit, which would give him time to get the lantern? Or would they give up the chase and go after Mr Bazalgette? Would they even remember the lantern?

Prising away another piece of wood, Topher felt glad that Streak was tied up, though he could hear the dog howling with frustration.

As more wood came away in his hand he heard an angry whisper. 'Blast! The cat's seen us.'

'What d'ya expect?' That was Army.

'But she's not scared.' Quiltie lowered his voice. 'See, she's still sitting there. Puss, puss, pretty pussy. No, don't go.'

She must have moved further away because now Topher couldn't see her. But he could see Quiltie creeping up on her.

'Pussy, pussy, nice pussy cat. Not that way, this way.'

Clever Ka. She was drawing them away from the lantern, and making them think they had a chance of catching her. He tore off another piece of wood, making a hole big enough for his hand, but not wide enough to pull the lantern through, not yet. And he mustn't take it too soon. Not while the Rookery coves were there. What if one of them turned round? But what if Ka was waiting for him to get the lantern before she made a run for it, leading them away? Topher pulled off another bit of wood. Now the hole was big enough.

'Ow! Blasted cat got me!'

Ka was giving him his chance.

Quickly he pulled the lantern through the gap he'd made, careful not to knock out the light. Then he turned away, hiding the light with his body, and waded back to the stinking sewer.

Someone above him swore. The dog howled. Ka was still creating a diversion.

'After her!' yelled Quiltie.

Feet pounded over the planks.

But not Army McAvoy's. 'Nah,' he growled. 'It's no use. Now where's that lantern?'

As Topher crouched in the mouth of the stinking sewer he feared for his life. If Army McAvoy found him now, he was dead.

Chapter 21

Army was still up on the bridge.

Topher, bent double in the stinking sewer, heard him stomping around.

'I know I put it here somewhere.' The stomping changed to a shuffling as if he were crawling about, feeling for the lantern with his hands. 'Blast. Remember putting it down. Must have fallen through that hole.'

Topher prayed the cove wouldn't start thinking someone had pinched it.

'Blasted dog must have sent it flying.'

Phew! That's right, blame the dog.

More stomping. The bridge creaked. But would Army come down the bank to look for it? Or decide to set off again for Mr Bazalgette's house without it? Where were the others? Where was Ka? Topher's head was full of questions.

'Ouch!' Topher flinched as the side of the lantern burned his skin. He'd been holding it close while facing the side of the sewer, trying to hide its light.

Had Army heard his cry? He tried to keep the lantern covered as he waited. For several minutes he strained his ears for the sound of footsteps or voices, but all he could hear was water lapping, the wind sighing and sometimes the hoot of an owl. There was no more stomping. No more creaking. Army didn't come down the bank. Either he was standing very still or he'd gone.

Topher waited a bit longer before deciding that Army had gone. To Mr Bazalgette's most like, if he could find his way there without the lantern.

So what should he do now?

First he stepped out of the sewer and breathed. He took in great gulps of fresh night air to try and get rid of the stink in his nostrils. Then he stood on tiptoe so he could see up and down the road. He didn't want to climb the bank. Not yet. Not till he'd checked the way was clear. Then he thought he heard a miaow. It seemed to come from the bridge. Cautiously he waded towards the sound and there she was, Ka!

Miaow! She was looking down through the hole he'd made.

Prrrt. She jumped onto his shoulder and rubbed her cheeks against his face, making soft chirruping sounds of pleasure. But not for long.

'*Hu...rrr...y.*' She stared at the round mouth of the sewer.

'Not back in there?'

'*Hu...rrr...y. Hu...rrr...y,*' Ka insisted.

Mouth was the wrong word, Topher thought as he stepped inside. It was like the other end of some stinking monster. The stench, bad at the start, got worse as they went further inside. Soon rats kept them company, scurrying along the water's edge, bold, even when they saw Ka on his back. The rodents' giant shadows jerked along beside them. So did his own. Bent double, he looked like a hunchback. Further in, even more rats were sitting twitching their whiskers on cushions of a weird yellow fungus that coated the brickwork. Then one sprang.

Topher raised his hand to repel it, but Ka was quicker. He watched the rat's plump, brown body plop into the sludge around his shins. Dead, with blood on the back of its neck, it made slow ripples in the filth.

'Th-thanks, Ka.' Rat bites were fatal. She had probably saved his life.

'*Hu . . . rrr . . . y. Hu . . . rrr . . . y.*'

But it was getting harder to hurry. The sludge was thicker. Was this really a short cut to Mr Bazalgette's house? He began to have his doubts and he felt Ka stiffen. Was another rat about to spring? He froze but she didn't move. Ears pricked, she was listening, so he listened too and heard a rushing sound.

At first he thought it was the sound of someone flushing one of these newfangled water closets, or several people even, for the water was getting deeper. But then he felt it pushing against his legs from behind. Suddenly it was above his knees. Oh, no! High tide! It must be. Now Topher remembered how the water rushed along the Thames from the estuary. He knew it rushed into its tributaries too, but he hadn't realised how far it surged, or how fast.

'How much further, Ka?'

She didn't answer and he wondered if the cat knew how to get out? Now he was moving faster, helped by the water pushing at his back, but a dreadful thought came into his head. *How deep does it get?* The water was rising inches every minute now. Holding the lantern high for a moment, he saw there were no dry areas. The brickwork was damp right up to the roof. If they didn't get out soon they would drown. He could see even more water oozing in from pipes to the side of the sewer, and he felt it dripping onto the back of his neck. Looking up, Topher saw grates above them. Grates – so there must be roads above and gutters full of rain. They must have reached a built-up area, but had they reached St John's Wood?

Mwow! The sound of rushing water made it hard to hear and there were more noises above. Ka pawed his cheek to get his attention. Carts and cabs were rattling overhead. He could hear the clip-clop of horses' hooves and the cries of street sellers.

'Read all about it! Read all about it!'

'*Hu…rrry.*' Ka spoke urgently into his ear but he didn't need urging. The water was rising fast.

'Lovely hot chestnuts! Tuppence a bag!'

'Mutton pies! Mutton pies!'

Food! So near but so far away! How on earth were they going to get out of here?

'*Sss… top.*' Ka hissed in his ear.

Pausing, Topher saw a metal ladder that came down from the road fixed to the wall of a shaft. Raising the lantern, he saw a round manhole cover at the top. Ka was looking up at it.

'You want me to open it?'

Hooking the lantern over his arm, he grasped the sides of the ladder, recoiling at the feel of slime on his hands. Then, forcing himself to grasp it again, he started to climb with Ka wrapped round his neck. But when he got to the top and pushed the cover nothing happened.

'*Tu . . . rrr . . . n.*'

'Turn it?' Topher tried to but it still didn't budge. He tried again but his arms ached.

'*Otherrrr way.*'

He tried to do as she said. Still the cover didn't budge. Then he tried pushing it again. He pushed till there was no more strength in his arms. He pushed till tears ran down his cheeks. Only then did he look down, see the water half-way up the ladder, rising fast, and realise they were trapped.

Chapter 22

'Help! Help!'

But no one heard Topher's cries. The shouts of street sellers were much louder than his frail voice, already weak with hunger. And when the rain got heavier and the street sellers went home no one else lingered to listen. Now the manhole cover clanged like a funeral bell as folk hurried past.

A church clock struck the half-hour, then the third quarter, then the hour. Nine o'clock. They were probably too late anyway. Snoop and co would have reached Mr Bazalgette's by now.

'*Trrr...y again.*' Ka was draped round his neck like a muffler.

Again he pushed against the cover, water dripping onto his head where it didn't fit too well. Again he cried for help. He cried till his throat was raw. From above Topher heard, 'Foul weather,' and 'All right for ducks,' and other scraps of talk that made no sense at all, but no one seemed to hear him.

'Looks as if we're going to die here, Ka.'

'*Trrr...y,*' she growled.

He opened his mouth but no sound at all came out. Then he had an idea. Sliding the lantern off his arm, he held it high, propping it on the top rung of the ladder, and minutes later he heard a toff's voice say, 'There's a light down there.'

'Must be a tosher or a flusher,' another replied.

'At this time of night?'

'They work all hours. I've heard tell some of them sleep down there.'

'*Help!* Let – me – out!' Topher forced the words from his mouth, and they cut his throat like razor blades.

Miaow! Ka joined in.

'A cat too,' said one gentleman.

'Might be that missing one.'

'Better get a peeler then, or the watchman.'

'Mmmm. We're rather late for dinner. More like it's a moggy.'

'*HELP!*' Topher made another desperate cry, but heard their footsteps grow fainter. Would they come back? Would they bring help? Why hadn't they lifted the cover themselves? Because they didn't want to dirty their hands, he supposed, fine gentlemen like them. And what if they did come back with a peeler? Was that good or bad?

'What do you think, Ka?'

'*Rrrrrr ... un. Rrrr ... un.*'

'Run? Got to get out of here first. But won't it be best to tell the peeler about the plot to kill Mr Bazalgette? Then he'll know I'm a good cove?'

'*Rrrr ... un.*' Ka sat upright on his shoulder now, as if ready to jump out as soon as the cover was lifted.

'But wouldn't the peeler go straight to his house and warn him?'

'*Rrrr ... un.*'

Ka seemed certain. Topher didn't know. Didn't care right at this moment. The filthy water was up to his thighs now. Even being arrested would be better than this. The tide must still be coming in, bringing waves of the terrible stink as well as the water. Could you die from the smell? What would be worse, that or drowning?

Then footsteps broke into his gloomy thoughts! His hopes rose, but sank again when they didn't stop.

More footsteps! More voices! They'd stopped!

But what for? Who was there? Straining his ears, Topher thought he recognised the voices he'd heard earlier along with another Cockney voice, and soon after that he definitely heard a grating sound. Looking up, he saw the manhole cover slowly moving. He saw a peeler's helmet, then a top hat, then two top hats. Three faces looked down briefly before recoiling at the stink.

'Cor blimey!' The peeler held his nose. 'But I do believe that is Cappelli's cat. So the ragamuffin with him is the thief, no doubt.'

'No,' said Topher. 'I'm not.'

'The cat does seem attached to the boy,' said one of the gentlemen. 'Listen, it's purring.'

But Ka wasn't purring. Ka was talking.

'*Rrrr...un.*'

'Please, sir,' Topher tried again. 'I'm not a thief, sir. We're on our way to Mr Bazalgette's, sir, to warn him...'

But no one was listening.

'Isn't there a reward for the return of this creature?' asked one of the gentlemen.

'There most certainly is,' said the other. 'What can we put it in?'

'My portmanteau?' He placed a large leather bag on the ground.

'That should hold it,' said the peeler. 'You take care of the cat, gentlemen. I'll see to the boy. Come on out, lad.' He held a hairy hand towards Topher. 'You're coming with me.'

'*Rrrrrrrrr . . . un. Rrrrrrrrr . . . un.*' Topher could feel the tension in Ka's body. Feel her claws digging into his shoulder. She was getting ready to spring.

He tried once more. 'Please, sir, Mr Bazalgette's life is in danger, sir. Armed men are on the way to his house.'

The clock struck the quarter-hour.

'They want to murder him.'

But the peeler wasn't listening. Now Topher saw handcuffs dangling from his other hand. The toffs weren't listening either. Intent on catching Ka, one was holding the portmanteau on its side. The other was positioning himself to block the remaining space around the manhole with his legs.

But Ka had no intention of being caught. Topher felt the thrust of her hind legs as she sprang.

'Jumping Jehosaphat!' The peeler swore as the cat shot between his legs.

And Topher followed, first on hands and knees then running upright.

'Stone the crows! Fast as lightning!'

'Stone the little guttersnipe!' yelled the peeler.

As something hit the back of his legs, Topher kept running after Ka, hoping she knew where she was going. He saw the peeler's helmet bowling past him. Heard his whistle blowing. Soon after that another peeler appeared in front, blocking their path.

'Stop in the name of the law!'

What now?

Ka dived into an alley on their right.

Topher followed. Head down he ran and ran though he couldn't see the cat. Then he could. Her green eyes shone from the darkness. He caught up with her, crouching by a wall and she hissed urgently.

'Ssss . . . ilent.'

Topher kept as quiet as he could, hunching down, too exhausted to move, his breath coming in gasps. A search was on. There was no doubt about that. Police whistles blasted, shouts echoed down the alleys, footsteps pounded the cobbles. It sounded as if there were peelers everywhere.

After a bit Ka sprang onto a wall and lay flat. Topher wished *he* could too. The only good thing about this mess was that if Snoop and co were near they must be able to hear the hullabaloo. Surely they wouldn't stay around with so many peelers about?

The noise seemed to go on for ages, but no one came down the alley where they were hiding, and at last all went quiet.

'Ssss . . . tay.' Ka walked along the top of the wall surveying the territory and Topher hoped they were near Hamilton Terrace. He was too exhausted to walk much further.

Miaow! Ka was back.

Cautiously he followed her out of the alley across some grass and into a tree-lined street full of smart new houses. Light shone from front-parlour windows and some basements. Good! because Topher realised he'd left the lantern in the sewer. Brass doorknockers gleamed. A street sign showed up clearly against a clean white wall. Hamilton Terrace! What a clever cat! Where was number 17?

Topher stepped forward nervously. There seemed to be no one about, but there were plenty of places to hide. Snoop could easily be out of sight behind one of the trees or even above him in the branches.

Miaow! Ka stood at the bottom of a flight of steps leading to one of the houses.

Number 17! He could see it engraved on a shiny brass plaque beside the door. Topher climbed the steps as quickly as he could and leaned on the bell push as Ka rubbed against his legs. He heard a bell ringing inside the house. *Come on. Come on.* But no one came. Why not? He rang again. Ka jumped onto the railings beside the steps and then onto the windowsill of the front parlour.

Still no one came to the door.

Miaow! Ka drummed the windowpane with her paws – and someone came to the window! Mr Bazalgette himself! Those bushy eyebrows were unmistakable.

'Open the door! *Please!*' Now Topher saw that there was a dinner party going on. At the table was a face he recognised – Miss Florence Nightingale's. He'd know her likeness anywhere. He'd seen it on so many stolen trinkets. But Miss Nightingale wasn't holding a lamp or looking tenderly at a wounded soldier. She was distracted by a bird on her shoulder, a cream-coloured owl.

Mr Bazalgette pushed up the sash window. 'Cappelli's cat!'

'My owl! Close the window!' Miss Nightingale shrieked.

Turning back to the door, Topher pressed the bell again, and nearly fell inside as the door was opened by a housemaid in a black dress and white mob cap.

'Playing knock down ginger, ragamuffin? Well run away now!' She pushed him back out of the door and slammed it shut.

Then Topher heard a sniggering laugh behind him.

'Gotcha, Toffee!'

Chapter 23

Snoop was at the bottom of the steps.

'I've got Slim, so you'd better do as I say. Start walking down.'

Topher looked quickly left and right but he couldn't jump over the railings like Ka had done. Or slide through them. Where *was* Ka?

'Come on down, Toffee.'

Something shuffled below in the basement yard. Topher guessed it was Mr Wiggins with his cosh.

'Yes, we've got you covered, Toffee.' Snoop put one foot on the bottom step.

Topher started walking towards him, but as slowly as he could, trying to think of an escape route. When a triangle of light appeared in front of him he stopped, realising the door behind had opened again.

'Who was that, Alice?' A man's voice. 'I thought I recognised a boy outside.'

'Only a ragamuffin, sir,' the maid replied. 'I've sent him on his way.'

A hand came through the railings and Topher froze as it grabbed his ankle.

Wiggins whispered, 'Yell for help, Toffee, so the kind gentleman comes to your rescue.'

'Glock!' Snoop hissed back, 'He'll think I'm harming the blighter and get me.'

'You yell then,' said Wiggins, keeping hold of

Topher's ankle. 'Quick! Before he closes the door.'

And Snoop suddenly covered his head as if defending himself from blows. 'Help! *HELP!* I'm being attacked! Get off, you blighter! Get off!'

Topher didn't know what to do. Was Mr Bazalgette falling for this ruse? He turned to look, trying to break free from Wiggins. 'Don't come! It's a trap!' He managed to yell.

But Snoop increased his efforts. 'Help! *HELP!*' He was rolling around on the ground now.

Mr Bazalgette took a step down and Topher saw the cudgel in Wiggins's raised hand. The brute was standing by the steps ready to bang Mr Bazalgette on the back of his head as he passed.

'GO INSIDE! GET THE PEELERS!' As Topher forced out the words, he heard footsteps. Running footsteps. Looking up he saw Quiltie, Army McAvoy and another cove – the third one who had been with them on the bridge – coming into the street. Streak was ahead of them, barking madly.

Wiggins let go of Topher's ankle. But Snoop rolled towards him and grabbed the other one.

'GET OFF ME, TOPHER ROWLEY! HELP!'

Then Army was lurching towards them both, arm raised.

'Get out of the way, Snoop!'

As one villain let go of his ankle, Topher felt another deliver a crushing blow to the side of his head.

Opening his eyes he saw angels looking down on him.

He was lying on a puffy white cloud. He was in Heaven.

'He's waking up!' whispered an angel with dark curly hair and blue eyes.

'Thanks be to God,' said a taller angel with neat hair, parted in the middle and a white cap. 'Sleep, young man.' She wet his lips with something cool. 'When you wake in the morning you'll feel better.'

But when he opened his eyes again it wasn't morning, it was dark, and he didn't feel better. Now he thought he might be in hell. His head hurt as if it were being pounded with red-hot hammers. Suddenly a flame shone out of the darkness. He looked up expecting to see a red demon with horns and a tail but there was the angel, the tall one with the white cap. She wore a long black dress too and had hold of his wrist.

'Quiet, child, I am taking your pulse.' Her fingers were cool and there was silence while she counted. Then she let go of his arm and laid it gently on the white counterpane. 'It is getting slower and stronger. You are improving. Now, let me plump up your pillows.'

Pillows? Topher glanced to the side as the angel leaned over him. Yes, pillows, lovely soft pillows. Not puffy white clouds. It felt as if there was a feather mattress beneath him too.

'How is your head, child?'

'It hurts.' He closed his eyes to try and take the pain away.

'More laudanum, I think, doctor?'

Sensing someone else in the room, Topher opened his eyes and saw a man at the end of the bed. Then he thought he recognised the angel, who had an owl on her shoulder, a real owl with a heart-shaped face and round eyes. Suddenly memories rushed into his head...fine folk inside the house...murderers outside... Snoop... Wiggins with the cudgel...Oh, no! He tried to sit up.

'I've...got to warn...!' He tried to get his legs out from beneath the sheets. 'Mr Bazal...' But the sheets were tightly tucked in and strong hands were pushing him back against the pillows.

'You did warn me, lad,' said a gruff voice. 'You saved my life. Look, here I am.' And there was the man himself, Mr Bazalgette, standing next to a smiling round-faced lady and a little girl with curly black hair and eyes as blue as bluebells.

'Maria recognised you and the cat,' said the round-faced lady.

Ka! How could he have forgotten her? Where was she? Before he could ask, the lady with the owl was spooning something cool between his lips and his mouth was filled with sweetness. Was that really a fire burning in a shiny grate? Were those really flowery curtains at the windows? Was the sheet under his nose really scented with lavender? With his head full of questions he felt himself floating...

When he woke up again the pain in his head had gone.

'Are you ready for breakfast?' The plump-faced lady seemed to sail towards him in her billowing skirt. 'If you are I'll call Alice.' She pulled a cord that hung beside his bed.

He heard a bell tinkling in the distance. He saw he was wearing a striped flannel nightshirt.

'It is my elder son, Joseph's,' said the lady. 'I am Mrs Bazalgette. Yes? You understand now? Well, when Miss Nightingale had cleaned the wound on your head she insisted that you were washed and dressed in clean garments before being put to bed. She is passionately fond of hygiene.'

'Miss . . . ?'

'Nightingale? Yes, the famous nurse herself. Wasn't it fortunate that she was making one of her rare social calls? The great lady is almost a recluse these days, but she had honoured us by coming to dinner. Ah, here's Alice.'

The maid, the same one who had shooed him away from the door, came in with a tray and put it on the coverlet in front of him. 'Who's the lucky one, then?'

'Good question, Alice. This young man saved your master's life and we don't even know his name.'

'Well then, what's your moniker then?' Alice stood by the bed, white cap askew on hair the colour of conkers. 'Tell the mistress.'

But Topher was looking at someone else who had followed the maid into the room, two someone elses, a dark-haired girl and a cat. Ka jumped onto the bed, purring like an engine.

'Well, my name's Maria,' said the girl. 'Don't you remember me? Your cat does.'

'Y-yes, I'm Topher.' But the day they'd first met seemed an age away. 'She hid under your mother's skirt when she was escaping from Signor Cappelli.'

Alice lifted a silver lid from a plate of buttered toast. 'Eat up before that cat has it. Shoo!' She flapped a linen napkin at Ka, who just looked at her disdainfully.

Topher laughed and tore off a corner of toast. Then he fed it to Ka even though his mouth was watering. As she nibbled from his fingers Mrs Bazalgette looked the other way, but Alice said, 'Make the most of it while you can, cat. Signor Cappelli's coming round to fetch you later.'

'NO! HE CAN'T!' Topher's shout made Alice drop the silver lid. He couldn't believe what she had said. Just when he thought his troubles were over!

'She's not going back there ever!'

'Be calm, Topher,' said Mrs Bazalgette, trying to push him back against the pillows. 'The cat is Signor Cappelli's property.'

Chapter 24

'But he's cruel.'

Maria listened open-mouthed as Topher told them what Signor Cappelli did to his cats. Then she went running from the bedroom saying, 'I knew Ka had a good reason for hiding that day. I could see it from the look in her eyes. That's why I didn't tell Papa where she was, but I will tell him now!'

But would Mr Bazalgette care? Topher wondered. The man had a reputation for kindness to children but was he interested in kindness to animals?

Maria was soon back. 'Just in time,' she gasped. 'Papa was about to leave for work.'

'No I was not.' The great man came into the room. 'Maria, you must stop dramatising the situation. Let's stick to facts. I was first of all coming to see my rescuer.'

Mr Bazalgette came to the side of the bed. 'Topher, I thought you would like to know that arrests have been made. I have heard from the police. McAvoy, Wiggins, and that rapscallion Snoop are at Bow Street awaiting charges, and it's all thanks to you.'

'But what about Mr Squittle?' said Topher, suddenly realising that Mr Bazalgette was still in danger. 'And Mr Markely?'

'Squittle?' Mr Bazalgette raised one of his remarkably bushy eyebrows. 'Markely? Who are they?'

As quickly as he could, Topher explained about the plot to murder Mr Bazalgette. 'And they could try again. They *will* try again, I'm sure of it. If Mr Squittle can't arrange it Mr Markely will find someone else to do it. You mustn't go outside till they have been arrested too.'

Mrs Bazalgette grasped her husband's arm. 'Joseph, we must send word to Scotland Yard straight away.' She left the room.

The gentleman nodded. 'Send a servant, my dear. Topher, you have been very courageous, but are you brave enough to testify against these scoundrels?'

'Yes, sir. I think I am.'

'Even so, it will be your word against theirs, you know. The courts may find it hard to convict without more evidence.'

'There is the Duke of Northumberland's silver, sir. I know where that is hidden. If the peelers go to the Rookery in Cockspur they will find it. Will that be proof enough?'

Mr Bazalgette noticed the maid in the corner, listening to every word. 'Alice, hurry and tell your mistress to also inform the police about the silver.' Then he took Topher's hand. 'How can I ever repay you for saving my life, lad?'

'By saving Ka's?' The cat was under the bedclothes now and Topher could feel her warm fur against his leg. 'Please, sir, don't let her go back to Cappelli's.'

The great man looked concerned. 'But she is Signor Cappelli's property.'

'And he's a cruel monster!' cried Maria. 'I have told you what he does!'

'Maria, curb your exuberance.' Mrs Bazalgette had come back.

But Maria was irrepressible. 'Papa, didn't you tell me that there is now a Royal Society for the Prevention of Cruelty to Animals? Isn't Queen Victoria herself the patron? What would she say if she knew about this? Papa, you can tell her when you go to the palace!'

'My dear child, her majesty is patron of the Society to Prevent the Use of Climbing Boys also and I hear say there are still lads sweeping the chimneys of Windsor Castle.'

'But, Papa, you did say you wanted to give Topher a reward for saving your life.' Maria clung to his arm.

'All I ask is that you do not give Ka back to that man,' said Topher. Then he sank back against the pillows, still woozy from the laudanum they'd given him to dull the pain in his head.

Mr Bazalgette sighed. 'I will do my best. The man may be persuaded to accept payment in lieu of Ka. If he is as cruel as you say, he should be stopped. But, Topher, isn't there something else you would like? Something for yourself? A chance to earn an honest living perhaps?'

Topher nodded. It was what he wanted most in the world.

'Well, I have a proposal,' Mr Bazalgette told him. 'How would you like to help me make London a much better place to live in? How would you like to become an engineer and help rid, not just London but all the big cities of sickness and disease? I have invitations from people across the world asking me to make their cities healthier by constructing sewage systems. I cannot get to all these places myself so I need to train more engineers, lots of them, to help with the work. If we can clean up the cities and create clean water supplies we will rid the world of cholera and a plethora of other diseases.'

Rid the world of cholera! That alone would be wonderful!

'How about it?' Mr Bazalgette prompted. 'Do you want to help create a better world?'

'Yes, sir, I do.' As Topher spoke, Ka poked her head out from under the covers and began to purr. *Rrrrrrr. Rrrrrrr.* She sounded as if she approved. Maria clapped her hands.

Soon afterwards the little girl left the bedroom with her mother and father but returned shortly. 'I have asked Papa to tell the RSPCA about Signor Cappelli and he has asked me to entertain you while he does.' She put a picture card on the counterpane in front of him. It had pieces of string attached to two of its sides, which Ka grabbed hold of. 'See, there's a horse on one side and a fence on the other. Now, if Ka will let go of the strings I'll make the horse jump over the fence.' Maria managed to get the strings from the cat and wind them around her fingers. Then she flicked her wrists so the card spun – and the horse really did look as if it was jumping over the fence. 'See, a moving picture! Have a go. You need to be good with your hands if you are going to help Papa.'

Topher soon had the card spinning.

'Now, can you count?' Maria was putting more picture cards on the bed. 'Papa says it's no fault of yours if you can't, but I must teach you.'

'I can count.' He'd needed to be able to count shirts and buttons and reels of thread to stop the overseer diddling his mother.

'Count those then.' Maria pointed to the line of cards now on the counterpane. She was a *very* bossy little girl.

'Twenty-three.'

'Good. Now, this set of cards is called a myriorama or endless landscape.'

Side by side in a long row the cards made a picture of a country scene. It reminded Topher of happy times, when he'd lived in the village with his family. The memory brought tears to his eyes. It was odd how happy memories made him sad, but Maria didn't seem to notice.

'How many different pictures do you think one can make out of these twenty-three cards?'

'I've no idea.'

She pointed to a number on the packet. 1,686,553,615,927,9222,354,187,720.

'It's billions or even trillions. Papa can say the number and show you the mathematics. Engineers have to be good at mathematics, so you will have to learn. Now you make a picture.'

Topher made several, combining the cards in

different ways. Then Mrs Bazalgette came in and took Maria downstairs, telling her that Topher must rest.

It was quiet when the little girl had gone, and blissful to sink into the soft pillows and close his eyes. Ka settled on top of the counterpane, just below his chin, and began to purr. She sounded contented, but was she really safe? Mr Bazalgette had said he would *try* and pay off Signor Cappelli. Maria said her father would tell the RSPCA about him, but would they do anything about it?

With his head full of worrying questions Topher must have somehow fallen asleep, because when he opened his eyes, the sky outside was a fiery red.

Tee-whit. A sharp screech drew his attention to the end of the bed where an owl was staring at him. Had Miss Nightingale returned? He cast his eyes around the room, expecting to see the lady, but she wasn't there. Then he noticed that the flowery curtains were flapping and the window was open. Had the bird flown in?

Tee-whit. Round eyes shone from its heart-shaped face. The bird, the *huge* bird – it must have grown – stared at him. Then it turned slowly till it stood sideways facing the open window.

Tee-whit. Tee-whit.

Its cry woke Ka who turned to look at the bird, stretched, arched her back and started to walk towards it. Now the owl spread its wings so they opened like fans. The wing nearest to Ka was like a ramp and she ran up it. Suddenly Topher realised that she was smaller

133

than the bird. And, he caught sight of his own tiny hand on the counterpane, *so was he.*

'*Up. Up.*' Ka was sitting on the bird's back looking down at him.

He had to clamber over the hills and dales of the counterpane to reach the bird, whose wing was like a steep slope in front of him. As he began to climb, grasping the feathers with his hands, he felt them part beneath his fingers then spring back and when he was half-way up, the bird raised its wing and tipped him gently onto its back so that he landed behind Ka.

'*Hold tight.*' He had never heard the cat speak so clearly.

He put his arms round the bird's neck and felt it tense beneath him. Then there was a whoosh of wings and a surge of energy as it took off through the window into the busy street. *Over* the busy street. Topher saw people below but no one looked up to see him, a boy flying on an owl's back. Too late now, if they did look up, for he had gone. Already he was over a patch of green, Regent's Park he thought, but that shrank rapidly as the bird gathered speed and height. Now the landscape below was like one of Chapman and Hall's new maps, a pattern of lines and patches. Black lines, like the spokes of a wheel, slashed the green that surrounded the city. They must be the new railways, converging on London. There was the River Thames winding like a snake, but as he watched, the map below him was blurring. Colours faded and he felt very tired.

Darkness was falling and there were stars ahead, but still the bird rose higher. Up and up it went, faster and faster, till he was surrounded by stars. Balls of fire, they glimmered and flared. Shooting stars crossed their path. Dazzled by their brilliance and lulled by beating wings he closed his eyes and travelled on, zooming, unaware as the bird broke through barriers of space and sound and time and dimensions he couldn't name, carrying him back to his life in the twenty-first century.

Chapter 25

'*What* are you doing up there?' said a nurse in bright-blue trousers and a matching top. 'Why have you opened the window?'

A glance told Topher he was back in the twenty-first century hospital. Inside the intensive-care room, he was standing on the windowsill where the bird must have tipped him, but – he checked again – he had reverted to his normal size. *Phew!*

The nurse reached up for his hand. 'Let's get you back into bed, then I'll close that window.'

Once there, he saw a creamy-white bird flying away into the inky sky and he thought of Florence Nightingale. Was that really her owl flying back to her?

'What was the matter with me?' he asked later when Staff Nurse Robins – she had a name badge on her top – was taking his temperature. She'd put a thermometer in his ear and now she was clipping an instrument to his finger. It was to count his pulse, she said.

How things had changed! He remembered Miss Nightingale's cool fingers holding his wrist. He remembered watching her pale lips move as she counted. This nurse wore bright-pink lipstick and her floppy fringe half-covered her eyes. Miss Nightingale would not have approved, he was sure.

'An infection of some kind,' the nurse replied. 'We're not sure yet, but you've certainly made an amazing recovery. Luckily you responded well to the antibiotics.'

'It wasn't cholera then?'

'No!' She laughed. 'What on earth made you say that? Cholera was wiped out years ago. Well, in most of the world. You haven't been abroad lately, have you?'

'No...' Topher didn't finish his sentence, first because she'd think he was mad if he said, 'But I've been time travelling', second because he'd just noticed the statue of Ka on the bedside table. Surely she'd travelled back to the present with him? He'd thought she must be hiding under the bed, waiting for a chance to get beneath the bedclothes. Had she travelled back to Victorian times with the owl?

For the rest of the day and quite a lot of the night, he kept his eye on the statue. When they moved him out of intensive care into a ward, he carried it himself, and placed it carefully on the locker beside his bed.

It was the first thing Ellie noticed the next day when she came to visit with his dad and Molly. 'I said it would help you get better.'

'It did but I wish I could see Ka herself.' Topher was very worried about her.

'Er...' Ellie went red. 'You will when you get out of here.'

'Is she at your house then?' He didn't know why he asked. He knew Ellie couldn't have seen her. None of them could have seen Ka for a while.

Ellie said, 'She's in the house somewhere but you know how she likes hiding.'

Molly looked confused. 'Whose house, Ellie? What do you mean? Ka didn't come to London with Topher.'

'Er...' Topher changed the subject quickly before Ellie started arguing. 'I want to learn more about Joseph Bazalgette when I'm out of here.'

'The sewer chap?' his dad asked.

Ellie groaned. 'OK, but you only need to ask *my* dad. He knows everything about him, remember in the car on the way home from the station? Now, are you going to be out of here by Saturday? That's when we're going to *Oliver!* to the matinee.'

'What day is it?' He'd lost all track of time.

'Tuesday. You've been in hospital for two and a half days.'

'I seem to have been away for ages.'

I have been away for ages.

Where was Ka? That's all Topher could think about. When his visitors had gone he watched the statue constantly but it remained stone all day and night.

Molly and his dad took him home from hospital next day, because he had recovered from the mysterious infection so quickly. Well, they took him back to the Wentworths' house because he said he wanted to stay with Ellie and go to see *Oliver!*

Luckily, as soon as they got there, Molly insisted that he go and have a rest, so he went upstairs to the bedroom and locked the door. Then he took the statue out of his pocket and put it carefully on the bedside table. 'Come back to me, Ka.'

And she did! He had never seen the transformation happen so fast. Suddenly the stone was glowing. He could feel the heat on his face as he knelt down to watch. As the gold grew brighter and brighter, the heat became so strong he had to move back. Then the white specks began to sparkle and cracks appeared along the black lines, turning into glossy black hairs. Stone became fur almost instantly! He didn't know which bit to focus on, so much was happening at once. Ka's golden ears grew velvet soft. Claws, like little silver cutlasses, sprang from her paws. White whiskers sprang from her face, and lastly she opened her mouth to reveal a triangle of pink edged by tiny white shiny teeth.

Mwow! Her amber eyes gleamed, and with a flick of her tail she sprang from the table onto the floor.

'Welcome home, Ka!'

The cat rubbed her furry cheeks against his hand, owning him with her scent glands. '*I'm yours, Tophe...rrr, you...rrrs.*'

'And I'm yours, Ka.'

When he went downstairs she followed him into the kitchen and he saw a ripple of relief run through all the Wentworths.

'Ah, there she is!'

'Where have you been, cat?'

'How...?' Molly looked even more confused, but she must have decided they were talking about Duo, who was also in the kitchen, because she didn't say any more about Ka. She and his dad left for Chichester after lunch, saying they'd come back on Sunday to get Topher.

On Saturday afternoon he went with all the Wentworths to see *Oliver!* in Drury Lane, but first they went for a walk along the Embankment. Mr Wentworth suggested it. As he talked about cement and concrete and bricks and how Joseph Bazalgette insisted on using the very best materials to ensure the massive construction was as safe as possible, Luke and Russell began a game of hide-and-seek.

Even Topher's attention wandered a bit to the pleasure boats full of tourists scudding along the river belching diesel fumes. And he remembered a time when boats, powered by wind or steam or oars, couldn't move at all, when they were stuck in the middle of the River Thames because it was so clogged with sewage. He remembered the rats and the flies and the people fleeing, but most of all he remembered the stink. The stink, there was stink everywhere in Victorian times...

Ellie nudged him. 'What are you wrinkling your nose for? Dad's asked you three times if you'd like to go and pay homage to your hero.'

'Don't exaggerate, Ellie, but I did just mention that there is a memorial to Joseph Bazalgette set in the wall a bit further along.'

Mr Wentworth led them to a row of memorials, like little shrines, set into the wall along the Embankment. Topher didn't recognise any of their names or faces, except Joseph Bazalgette's, and he was disappointed to see only his top half. He'd expected to see a huge statue of such an important man, but there was only Mr Bazalgette's head and chest. Made of bronze, it was surrounded by fancy stonework to make it look like a little Greek temple. But it didn't, well, *stand out* from all the others and Joseph Bazalgette had *stood out*. He wasn't a tall man but he was outstanding.

Ellie laughed. 'What a moustache! How did he drink with that?'

The moustache was even wider than Topher remembered, and the gentleman's head was balder. It looked like him, but as he must have looked when he was older, when he'd been knighted by Queen Victoria herself.

'Should be a huge statue, shouldn't there?' said Mr Wentworth, echoing Topher's thoughts. 'Like there is for Isambard Kingdom Brunel.'

'Exactly,' Topher agreed, but now Ellie was tugging at her dad's arm and Mrs Wentworth was looking at her watch.

'OK, darling. OK, Ellie, there's no need to pull my arm off. We'll go to the theatre now.'

Oliver! was great. Topher enjoyed it right from the opening chorus of 'Food, Glorious Food', but he couldn't help comparing it to real life in Victorian times. All they'd sung in the workhouse were dreary hymns, and they hadn't had the energy to dance or jump around. The *un*reality of it was probably why he enjoyed it, Topher reasoned. He didn't want to be reminded of his recent trip to Victorian London. All the bright lights on stage suited him fine. He didn't want to remember the dark alleys and air so thick you could hardly see a yard in front of you. He didn't want to see poor folk wearing dingy rags. All the colourful costumes cheered him up. He liked the actors' clean faces, some of them daubed with grease paint to look like dirt. He'd had enough of real dirt. He couldn't help laughing at Fagin, and the Artful Dodger and the rest of the thieves, loveable rogues all of them. Only cruel Bill Sykes sent a tremor of fear through him. He was a bit too much like Wiggins and Squittle and Army McAvoy.

When they got home Topher headed upstairs. 'To see Ka,' he said when Ellie asked, because it was partially true. He didn't say that he was actually going to do his holiday homework again. He knew what she'd say if he did. He couldn't quite believe it himself, but he'd gone off writing about Queen Victoria. She may well have influenced her times. She'd given her name to a whole era and lots of places. She'd done some good, but not as much good as a not-so-famous engineer. One man had spent his whole career trying to make life better for other people. He succeeded too. Billions of people had benefited from his work, and were still.

Ka was curled up on the bed but opened her eyes when Topher walked in.

'I'm going to write about the Great Stink of 1858 and how Joseph Bazalgette brought an end to it.'

'*Rrrrrr...*' She purred as he stroked her fur. '*Rrrr...ight. You're right.*'

Or had she said, '*Wrrr...ite*'?

For a while Topher rested his face on her soft fur, but then he picked up his pen to begin.

Glossary of Victorian words

billet	– sleeping place
billy	– handkerchief
busting	– breaking into houses
buzzing	– stealing
cosh	– weapon like a truncheon
cove	– man
daguerreotype	– a photograph
fence	– receiver of stolen goods
fine wirer	– a highly skilled pickpocket
glock	– half-wit, stupid person
hansom cab	– two-wheeled horse-drawn cab (inventor Joseph Hansom)
Jack Tar	– sailor
moniker	– name or signature
major-domo	– head servant in large household, manager
parlour jumping	– breaking into houses
plates of meat	– feet
peeler	– policeman
rookery	– slum or ghetto
smatterhauling	– stealing handkerchiefs

snowing	– stealing clothes from washing lines
spats	– covering for lower leg and ankle
spike	– workhouse
star glazing	– taking out a window pane and stealing goods
swell	– smartly dressed gentleman
tea leaf	– thief
toff	– a smartly dressed gentleman
togs	– clothes
wherry	– shallow boat, like a barge

Historical Note

Florence Nightingale really did have a pet owl, which she called Athena. She found it injured in the Parthenon in Athens, nursed it back to health and brought it home with her home to England. Sadly it died before she went to the Crimea – causing her great distress. My story takes place in 1858, after the Crimean War. I always strive for historical accuracy but in this story I have allowed myself one piece of poetic licence, allowing Athena to live a few years longer.

THE TIME-TRAVELLING CAT
AND THE
AZTEC SACRIFICE

JULIA JARMAN

Topher Hope is distraught when Ka, his devoted cat disappears, leaving a word on his computer:

TENOCHT*I*TLaN

Wasn't that the home of the blood-thirsty Aztecs? Then she must be in dreadful danger. But when Topher travels back to the time of the Aztecs, he finds trouble from another source. The Aztecs think Ka is one of their gods, but El Sol, a piratical Spanish conquistador, thinks she is a witch.

Can Topher save Ka from El Sol, rescue Pima, a girl the Aztecs want to Sacrifice, and escape from the wondrous, floating city of Tenochtitlan before it is destroyed?

'Fast moving adventure'
The Teacher

9781842705162 £4.99

THE TIME-TRAVELLING CAT
AND THE
EGYPTIAN GODDESS

JULIA JARMAN

Topher travels to Ancient Egypt in search of his cat, Ka, in this historical adventure.

Ka is the cleverest, most beautiful cat Topher has ever seen. She talks, writes on his computer –

B-+bast*is

– and travels through time to Ancient Egypt. But when Topher goes in search of her, he learns that she is going be sacrificed. Can he rescue her? Will the priestess, mysteriously like his mum who died in an air crash, help or hinder him?

'Intriguing fantasy'
Books for Keeps

9781842705216 £4.99

THE TIME-TRAVELLING CAT AND THE ROMAN EAGLE

JULIA JARMAN

Topher Hope is on the move again. When his devoted cat, Ka, leaves a computer message saying she has gone to

CA;;LLevA

he follows her to a Romano-British settlement in AD 79. Ka is happy among the cat-adoring conquerors with their central heating! Topher, now a British boy, apprenticed to a Roman mosaic maker, has mixed loyalties. When the eagle, symbol of Roman power, disappears from the forum, the fragile peace is threatened. Topher begins a desperate search, and he needs all the amazing powers of the time-travelling cat.

'Recreates life in Romano-Britain with vividness and ease . . . An enjoyable story.'
Books For Keeps

9781842706176 £4.99

THE TIME-TRAVELLING CAT
and the Tudor Treasure

JULIA JARMAN

Ka, the time-travelling cat, has disappeared, leaving just one clue – a word on Topher's computer screen:

R*iche mou*nt

When Topher discovers that 'Richemount' meant 'Richmond' in Tudor times, he fears that Ka is in terrible danger. Cats were tortured in Tudor England, so Topher must try to find her before it is too late. In doing so, he meets Queen Elizabeth and Doctor Dee, the court magician and astronomer, who thinks Ka can help him find the elusive philosopher's stone.

'A good read'
School Librarian

9781842706169 £4.99

THE TIME-TRAVELLING CAT AND THE VIKING TERROR

JULIA JARMAN

Topher is planning a trip to London to visit his friend Ellie – but will it be safe, with all the terrorist threats? It worries him, and so do the extended absences of his beloved cat, Ka. She is going travelling again, and Topher doesn't want to lose her. And sure enough, in the middle of a big bomb alert, Topher is called away – to a Saxon village threatened by Norsemen. Now he must protect the villagers from the terrifying Viking, Ingwar the Boneless, infamous for his cruelty and devious tricks.

'Jarman writes in an engaging manner revealing an exciting slant to history and *Viking Terror* is no exception.' *Write Away*

9781842706862 £4.99